She was going to make him sweat...

Beneath the oak boardroom table, Emma slid off her right high heel. Slowly she inched her stocking-clad foot toward Michael's leg.

He froze when she touched him. And stopped in midsentence, his face flushing pink. All the board members glanced quizzically in his direction.

Emma's foot next found Michael's knee, but didn't linger long. The knee held no interest. His inner thigh did.

As her foot continued on its journey, heat started to suffuse her body. Her breathing shallowed. *No, she wouldn't let herself be turned on by him.*

But as her foot inched toward the juncture of his thighs, her heart began pounding. She stopped, then swallowed hard. Carefully she zeroed in with her big toe, touching him *there.*

Michael's face reddened and he nearly choked. The other board members stared at him in open astonishment.

Emma grinned. She had him. Just where she wanted him. And it felt *good. Very good.*

Unfortunately too good for her own liking....

Jo Leigh is a native Californian currently living in Texas. Storytelling has always been a part of her life, whether as a producer in Hollywood, a screenwriter or a novelist. *One Wicked Night* is Jo's sixth published book, though she has several more in the works. Look for her next Temptation title, a Mail Order Men story, coming in the fall of 1998. Enjoy!

Books by Jo Leigh

HARLEQUIN AMERICAN ROMANCE
695—QUICK, FIND A RING!

SILHOUETTE INTIMATE MOMENTS
569—SUSPECT
659—HUNTED
740—EVERYDAY HERO

Don't miss any of our special offers. Write to us at the following address for information on our newest releases.

Harlequin Reader Service
U.S.: 3010 Walden Ave., P.O. Box 1325, Buffalo, NY 14269
Canadian: P.O. Box 609, Fort Erie, Ont. L2A 5X3

ONE WICKED NIGHT
Jo Leigh

Harlequin Books

TORONTO • NEW YORK • LONDON
AMSTERDAM • PARIS • SYDNEY • HAMBURG
STOCKHOLM • ATHENS • TOKYO • MILAN
MADRID • WARSAW • BUDAPEST • AUCKLAND

Thanks to Birgit Davis-Todd and Huntley Fitzpatrick for giving me a shot!

ISBN 0-373-25774-0

ONE WICKED NIGHT

Copyright © 1998 by Jolie Kramer.

Printed in U.S.A.

1

THE FIRST THING Michael Craig saw was her leg. Long, sleek and clad in a high-heeled black shoe, it was a leg that would have stopped him even if he hadn't been on the lookout for her. It was a leg that deserved attention.

He waited impatiently for the rest of the woman to emerge from the limousine. If the leg was this good, perhaps the rest of her was also more enticing than her grainy newspaper photograph had led him to believe. Shifting a bit to his left to get a better view, he watched as Emma Roberts leaned forward, her long straight dark hair obscuring her face. But only for a moment. She stood, and the hair fell back so he could see her profile. He wasn't close enough for details, but from here, she seemed attractive. Not quite as beautiful as the leg had promised, but not bad.

As she turned and he got a look at her from the front he revised his original assessment yet again. She looked younger than twenty-eight. Her somewhat severe black suit seemed incongruous on her, as if she were playing dress up. He looked once more at the newspaper photo in his hand. In it, Emma's hair was pulled back in a bun. That was the difference, of course. He hoped she would wear it back tonight. It would be a lot easier to do what he had to if she didn't look so innocent.

He watched her as the bellman came over and got her bags from the trunk. She stood very straight, with her toes pointed slightly out, a sure sign that she'd studied ballet. He'd gone out with a dancer once. Amazingly limber.

Emma turned to look at the twenty-six-story hotel before her. Then she turned his way and he saw she was smiling. Was it the architecture that pleased her? Or was it the fact that she was on an all expenses paid vacation courtesy of her company? Or maybe she'd never been to New Orleans before. He hoped she hadn't. He'd like to show her the city for the first time. Even if he didn't have enough charm to do the job, the city did. New Orleans could seduce the hardest hearts. Emma wouldn't stand a chance.

She walked toward the big glass door, but paused before entering. Slowly turning, she looked back at the limo, the street and finally she turned his way. He thought about ducking back, but what was the point? She didn't know him. There was no reason for her to think of him as anything but part of the scenery.

But that's not what happened. When her gaze came to him, it lingered. Just for a moment. In that moment, Michael got a strange feeling in the pit of his stomach. It had been a mistake, seeing her like this. He should have just waited until dinner and gone ahead with his plan. He wasn't sure, but he thought the strange feeling might just be guilt. No, he was probably wrong about that. There was no room for guilt in business. He who ends up with the most toys wins and Michael was determined to end up with the most toys. Including Emma Roberts.

EMMA LOOKED AROUND the elegant dining room and saw she was the only single party in the place. Single party. Party of one. Talk about oxymorons. She'd never felt less like a party girl, which was yet another example of how her dreams got her into trouble every time.

This was supposed to be the night of her life. She'd won this trip to New Orleans as Employee of the Year at Transco Oil. All expenses paid, dinner at this five-star restaurant, even the company jet to wing her from Houston and back again. Well, she made a lousy Cinderella. She'd been so excited—looked forward to this trip for weeks—and now, all she felt was lonely. Prince Charming must have had other plans.

She took another bite of salad, then stared at the flickering candle on her table. It was better than staring at the couples around her, all of whom seemed to be spectacularly, demonstratively, in love.

The tap on her shoulder startled her, but then she remembered she'd asked the waiter for the sommelier. She turned. And nearly choked on her lettuce. The wine steward was the single best-looking man she'd ever seen. He made the Diet Coke guy look like Barney Fife. The sommelier's dark hair was slightly wavy and thick and a bit long around the collar. His eyes sparkled, and he smiled elegantly with perfect teeth. And his jaw—she'd never been big on jaws before—but this one changed her forever.

"Ms. Roberts?"

Boy, he was good. How had he found out her name? She nodded, wanting him to speak again so she could get another shiver from that baritone voice of his.

"From Transco Oil?"

"Wow," she said. When he smiled, she realized she'd said it aloud. "I mean, wine. Wine, you know. To drink."

"Yes, I've heard of it." He said it gently, teasing. Then he snapped his fingers and at once a man wearing a corkscrew on a chain around his neck was at his side. "Puligny Montrachet, *s'il vous plaît*, Pierre."

Emma blinked. Twice. If Pierre was the sommelier... "Who are you?" she asked the man with the remarkable jaw.

"I'm Michael Craig. I read about you in the *Chronicle*. Congratulations on winning your prize. You must be very pleased."

Blinking seemed appropriate again. "You recognized my picture from a Houston paper?"

"Yes, of course. I never forget a pretty face."

That did it. The fantasy he'd created vanished as she realized the beautiful man was a liar. "Well, thank you," she said, now just wishing he'd leave. Hoping he couldn't see the rush of heat in her cheeks.

"You're quite welcome." He walked around the table and put his hand on the chair across from her. "I'm afraid I've been stood up. I see you've already ordered, but if it's not too presumptuous of me...may I join you?"

"I...uh..."

"Thank you."

He sat down, but not before she got a good look at his tuxedo. She'd never seen anything like it before. At least not in person. It fit him perfectly, accentuating his broad shoulders and slim waist. Good grief, who in their right mind would stand up this man?

"I was supposed to go to the opera with three men from Oklahoma. One of them goes by the name of Bubba Jorgenson. What a night it would have been, eh?"

Despite her earlier wish for Prince Charming to appear, Emma tried to figure out how to politely tell him that she'd rather dine alone. She was always fascinating to men who lived only in her mind. With the real thing, however...? On the other hand, he sure did improve the view. What the heck. One dinner with a beautiful liar wouldn't kill her. "Bubba Jorgenson? It's not a name one would forget."

Michael smiled. Oh, heavens. It was enough to set her heart racing. Why hadn't she listened to her friends? They'd begged her to go for a makeover, to get her hair done, to buy some new clothes. But no. She had waved all the poofery aside, and now here she was with Adonis himself, while she felt like a charwoman. Well, maybe not that bad. Although next to Michael, Cindy Crawford would get a complex.

"Now, you need to tell me what you did to become Employee of the Year. That's quite an honor."

If she hadn't been watching him, listening to the tone of his voice, she would have been certain he was being sarcastic.

"You really recognized me from that silly photo? I would barely recognize the president from a picture in the newspaper."

"Yes, I really did. The article is in my briefcase up in my room. If you'd like, I can go get it and show you."

She shook her head. "No, that's okay. I believe you...I think."

"Emma Roberts, head of research at Transco Oil of Houston was named Employee Of The Year at this year's annual meeting."

Emma recognized the words from the article. He'd memorized it verbatim.

"Philip Bailey, president and CEO of the privately owned natural resource company made the announcement on the heels of a disappointing third quarter...."

"Stop," she said, holding out her hand. "You win."

"Good. Then as my reward, I get to hear you answer my question."

"What question?"

"I asked what you did to win this grand prize."

"Oh, right. Well, it wasn't all that hard," she said. "All I had to do was show up for a full day's work every weekday for the past three years."

"That's real dedication."

She laughed. "That's real desperation."

"They don't pay you well at Transco?"

"Sure. The salary is fine. Except for the fact that I'm sole support for my mother and a sister who's in college."

The smile left, and his brow creased, which somehow made him better looking. "I'm sorry. That must be hard for such a young woman."

She shrugged, and sipped some water. After she put the glass down, she managed a smile of her own. "It's just life. No different from anyone else's. Well, maybe Madonna, but who'd want her problems?"

He laughed, and she knew right then if he asked her to make love with him right here on the dining room table, she'd say yes. Or at least maybe.

"It seems to me what you do must be very different from anyone else," he commented. "From what I read, I imagined your job would require someone unique."

"Actually, I head up the research department at Transco. My team and I coordinate resource exploration, expeditions and long-term feasibility studies." She felt her shoulders relax now that she was in familiar territory. "It's exciting."

"Not many people say that about their work. You must really enjoy it," he said.

"I do. I work with three of the best researchers in the business. We don't punch a time clock, we each have an area of expertise, and we get the job done."

"Satisfaction in a job well done," he said, his focus not on her any longer, but somewhere far away. "That's it, isn't it? What it's all about."

"You speak from experience?"

He was with her again. His eyes, a light hazel that contrasted with his tan skin, weren't dreamy anymore. They were serious, and interested and scanning her with acute intelligence. "I like to think so."

"What do you do?"

"I'm a businessman. But we're not here to talk about me. This is your night."

As if to emphasize his point the sommelier arrived just then and went through the ritual of wine acceptance with Michael. The label was examined, the cork popped, the liquid poured, then tasted. Emma and the steward waited for the nod of approval, and when it was given, her glass was filled.

Michael lifted his for a toast. "To a very lovely Employee of the Year," he said.

She lifted her own. "Bottoms up." She sipped just as he did, their gazes locked over their respective brims. By the time the wine reached her stomach, she was a goner. Before she could stop it an image of him taking off that Armani tux slid into her mind. The promise of what lay beneath elevated her temperature and kick-started her pulse.

"I'll have what the young lady is having," Michael said.

She hadn't noticed the waiter approach until she heard Michael speak.

"Would you like to begin with the salad, sir?"

"No, Emma will be fine."

Emma jolted back, then realized he'd said *entrée*, the *entrée* would be fine. The heat increased until she could feel her cheeks burn pink.

Michael turned to her when the waiter had gone. "Will you excuse me for a moment? I have to make a phone call."

She nodded and watched him walk away, wishing he would lift up the back of his tux so she could get a gander at what was underneath.

After he disappeared behind the door leading to the phones, she signaled the maître d'.

"Yes, ma'am?"

"The gentleman I'm sitting with. Do you know him?"

"Mr. Craig? Yes, of course. He comes here often."

"So he's not a crazed ax murderer or something?"

The maître d' laughed, and Emma felt her shoulders relax. "No, ma'am. He's a very good customer, and well-known in the hotel. I don't believe you have anything to worry about."

"Thank you," she said.

He nodded and walked away.

"But I'm not so sure," she whispered.

Then Michael appeared, and she was stunned once more at his elegance. It was ridiculous, really. He was just a man. Just like any other man. Uh-huh.

He sat down, flipping his napkin once and laying it on his lap. "This research," Michael said, as if there hadn't been a break in the conversation. "It's a lot of geology, isn't it?"

"That's my specialty. I have a master's degree in environmental geology. I look for alternate methods of oil extraction with an emphasis on preservation."

"That explains why Transco isn't doing too well."

"Oh?" He really did pay attention to the business section.

"Sure. They're not a slash-and-burn company. They have a stake in the planet. That costs money."

"But it's worth it, don't you think?"

"Of course. Up to a point."

"What point is that?"

"When they stop making a profit."

"Sometimes a profit isn't the goal," she said.

"It has to be. Or the job doesn't get done. The company goes under. No more responsible company watching out for the earth. It's a simple equation." He lifted his glass.

"It's only simple when you don't care."

The wine didn't make it to his lips. "A smart girl like you, and you think caring has something to do with success?"

"Don't you care about anything?"

"One thing only." He smiled again, but this time she wasn't so taken in by his looks that she didn't notice the slight sadness that came with it. "Profit."

"That's a strict master."

"I'm a practical man, Emma. I know that the best intentions without money remain intentions."

"A practical man in an Armani tuxedo? I don't think so."

"Pretty *and* observant," he said. "Very good."

"Well?"

"It's an investment. Plain and simple."

"It doesn't hurt that it makes you look superb, though, does it?"

"You think so?"

"No. *You* think so."

"Touché. But I'm disappointed. I was hoping the suit would give me bonus points."

"Don't worry. I think you're very pretty. Honest."

"Then spend the night with me."

That got her attention. She opened her mouth, then closed it again.

He laughed. "No, I didn't mean that. I meant the evening. We'll take a walk around Jackson Square. Maybe a ride in a carriage." He leaned forward and covered her hand with his. The sensation made her inhale quickly. Just looking at his hand, so wide and broad and masculine, made her feel suddenly feminine and cared for. It wasn't a feeling she was accustomed to.

"Please, Emma. New Orleans at night is quite something."

The waiter arrived, and Michael took his hand away. She couldn't have been less hungry, even though her scallops in wine sauce smelled wonderful. She wanted Michael to touch her again. Just once more. How had she gone so long without feeling like this? But still, he was a stranger. And she was, after all, Emma. "I don't think so. But thank you."

"You're worried. Which is a wise thing to be. These are dangerous times."

"Yes, I know."

"How can I convince you that I'm not like the times?"

"You? Not dangerous? There's no way I could ever be convinced of that."

He smiled and she found herself leaning forward.

"I have references," he said.

"What kind?"

"The manager of the hotel for one."

She shook her head. "Unless the manager is a woman, it's not going to be enough."

"Ah, so you think I have designs on you, is that it?"

A quick heat filled her cheeks and she looked away. What on earth had she been thinking? A man like that wanting her? Oh, sweet mercy she'd stuck her foot in it this time.

"Of course, you'd be correct," he said, his voice low, soft, intimate.

She gathered her courage and met his gaze once more. "Really?"

He laughed. "Why do you sound so surprised?"

"Because you're you, and I'm me."

The look he gave her was one she'd seen a hundred times before. She'd baffled him. He didn't know what to make of her. He found her...curious. It was her mouth, of course. Her inability to think before she spoke. Her foolish insistence on telling the truth had run off more men than she cared to think about, and now she was going to run off this magnificent specimen.

"Now, Emma, are we really so different, you and I?"

She laughed. "Yes."

"Why? We're both businesspeople. We're both in a city that isn't our home. We're intelligent, single and we both like scallops."

"Oh, well, I'd forgotten about the scallops. You're right. We're practically twins."

"And we both appreciate your sarcastic sense of humor," he said with a wry smile.

"Sorry. I don't mean to be—"

"Don't apologize. I do like it."

"You like smart-ass remarks?"

He nodded. "Much better than polite indifference."

"That puts the pressure on."

"Hmm?"

"Most of the time I don't think of the right smart-ass remark until the next day."

"Then it's a good thing I'm here for the whole weekend."

Emma went for her wineglass again. She concentrated on bringing it to her lips with a steady hand. Sipping, not gulping. Lord, was she out of her league here. The only thing she knew about men like Michael Craig was that they didn't go out with women like Emma Roberts. They dated beauty queens and fashion models. Not environmental researchers.

Finally, the light dawned. She swallowed a bigger gulp of wine than she had planned, and coughed, but thank God she didn't spit all over the table. The girls! Her three very nosy, very clever assistants at Transco had set this all up. It had to be. He was a paid escort! Of course. It all made sense now.

Ever thorough, the girls must have alerted the staff here at the hotel to play along. No wonder they'd wanted her to get the makeover. She was going to kill them on Monday. Imagine, hiring an escort to keep her company.

Now she looked at Michael with different eyes. Critical eyes. He must have cost a fortune. Richard Gere himself couldn't have played the part more convincingly. He was stunning, smooth, a good conversationalist. He even talked business like a professional. She had to hand it to them, they'd hired the best.

The only thing was, she didn't know what to do

now. Or how to feel. Should she be insulted? Or grateful?

"What's going on in that pretty head of yours?" Michael asked.

Should she play her hand? Let him know she'd figured out this little charade?

He leaned forward slightly. His gaze traveled over her face, feature by feature. She watched carefully for some indication of what he really thought of her. If this assignment was distasteful, or pleasant. She couldn't bear the former. He may be a paid escort, but he was still a man.

"I've been too forward, haven't I? I've made you uncomfortable."

She shook her head. "No, it's all right. You're just doing your job."

He leaned back. "My job?"

Emma decided right there that she wasn't going to let on. She was Cinderella, right? This was her night at the ball, and Michael was her Prince Charming. So he came with a price tag. What didn't these days? Knowing her friends, they'd checked him out up one side and down the other. She was safe, at least in the Boston Strangler sense of the word. But was it wise to play this fantasy out? To let herself be a princess for a weekend?

"Emma, what do you mean?"

"I was trying for smart-ass," she said. "But I got cryptic instead."

His eyes narrowed. "I'm not sure I understand."

"It's okay. It's nothing."

"You're not what I expected," he said, after a long pause.

She wondered briefly what the girls had told him about her. Probably extolled her virtues as a geologist and researcher. And, knowing them, they'd probably told him that she hadn't been on a date since the Hindenburg disaster. "What did you expect?"

"Someone a little more serious, a little more sedate."

"A scientist, right? Pocket protector. Thick glasses. Perhaps wearing an 'X-Files' T-shirt?"

He laughed. "No. Just not...you."

"You don't know the first thing about me, Mr. Craig."

"You're wrong, Emma. I've learned quite a bit so far."

"Oh?"

He moved his hand to hers once more. The touch undid her, made her stomach tighten, and she found herself crossing her legs.

"You're very bright," he said. "Maybe too bright for your own good. Because you're smart enough to see through the veneer, aren't you? You have things all figured out. You assume I want something. Well, you're right. I do. I want your company. No strings attached. I want to walk through New Orleans and see it through your eyes. I want to listen to your smart-ass remarks. And your laughter. Emma, come with me. Be mine, just for tonight."

It was now or never. She could put an end to the farce and tell him she knew he'd been hired to seduce her. Or she could let herself be seduced. She needed time to think it over, but of course there wasn't time. He wanted an answer. Now.

"All right," she said.

He cocked his head a bit to the side. "Really?"

She nodded. It was her night, wasn't it? So what if he was a hired prince? She wouldn't let it matter. Tonight, she would be Cinderella. Her real life would be there tomorrow, and a hundred tomorrows after that.

2

MICHAEL FELT inordinately pleased with himself. This was going better than he'd expected. While Emma wasn't exactly his ideal woman when it came to looks, she was pretty in her own way, and a quick thinker, which made his task very pleasant.

She didn't suspect a thing, that much he was sure of. Although for a moment there, he'd been afraid she was going to turn him down. It was clear she wasn't used to his kind of attention. She wore her skepticism like a cloak, and that, he thought, was going to be his biggest hurdle. Getting her to accept and believe that she was the most desirable woman in all of New Orleans wouldn't be easy. Luckily, he wasn't going to have to do too much acting.

He watched her sip her wine. He found himself wanting to touch her long and lovely throat. By caressing her hand, he'd already discovered how remarkably soft her skin was. Caution reigned, however, and he held back. He wasn't here to enjoy himself. He was here to find out about Transco Oil. To get the final details that would make his takeover of the company a fait accompli. Period.

If he did his job right, he'd have everything he

needed by the end of the night. Emma would be sadder, but wiser, and he'd be quite a bit richer.

"This is my first time in New Orleans," she said. "Can you believe it? I've lived in Houston all my life, and I've never come down here. I just kept meaning to."

"Then I'll show you the city."

"You're from here, then?"

He shook his head. "No, I live in Houston now. But I made it a point to visit New Orleans very early on."

"A real mover and shaker?"

"I don't procrastinate. Don't believe in it."

Emma played with a scallop on her plate for a minute. "So you just go after what you want? Just like that?"

He smiled. "Yep."

"How often do you succeed?"

He held back his first answer. Instead, he said, "Very often. But not always."

She put down her fork and touched her wineglass with her fingertips. He watched the way her hand moved, surprised at the delicate slip of her wrist. He hadn't thought she would be so slim. Or that he could be so taken by the small gesture.

"Do you still want what you can't have?" she asked quietly.

"No. Never. If it can't be mine, I walk away. No regrets."

"We're more alike than I'd imagined."

"How?"

"I walk away, too. Only I don't have the 'no regrets' part down yet. I envy you."

"Don't." He leaned forward, no longer able to watch her hand without touching it. He held it gently and rubbed her palm with his thumb.

"Why not?" she asked. "The regrets are the painful part."

"They're also the human part."

She looked away from his gaze to the interplay of their hands in the center of the white tablecloth. He continued to caress her palm and she watched the flickering candlelight play shadowy tricks.

"You surprise me, too," Emma said. "I thought I had you pegged. Now I'm not so sure."

He pulled away from her and took hold of his glass. "Ms. Roberts, I have the feeling you know exactly who I am." Then he turned, and signaled the waiter.

"Dessert for you and the lady, sir?" The waiter, who looked a little like John Lennon, leaned a bit forward, as if the answer to his question was a matter of great importance.

Michael looked at Emma, and she shook her head no. "We'll just take the bill," he said.

"That's already been taken care of, sir."

Once more, Michael turned to Emma. "Ready?"

This time she nodded yes.

Michael left a generous tip on the table, and then held Emma's chair for her. When she rose, the top of her head reached the bottom of his chin. He figured she must be about five foot five. Again, the delicacy of her body surprised him. She wore a soft pastel dress that clung to her as she walked, and beneath it he could see the outline of a slim, but womanly, figure.

She'd worn her hair down, and as he'd predicted it was making things more complicated. Just seeing how it framed her face, how it made her seem so pure and sweet, brought back that little niggling sensation he'd felt this afternoon. That wouldn't do. He thought of his profit and loss statement. His portfolio. There, that was better.

He put his hand on the center of her back, and he felt her body quiver at the touch. That was better, still. He was in control once more. Emma might be nice to touch, but he had an agenda, and that was all that mattered.

THE AIR OUTSIDE the restaurant was sultry and infused with the smell of the sea. It caressed Emma's face and arms and legs, and made her feel exotic and soft. She was incredibly aware of Michael's hand on the small of her back. It was warmer than human touch was supposed to be, the heat infiltrating her body and stirring her blood. She wanted him to move his hand away, and keep it there forever. She wanted to be safe, and yet she wanted adventure. Michael, she was sure, was more adventure than she'd had in her whole life.

"Let's walk this way," Michael said, nodding toward the river.

They walked slowly, Michael setting the pace. Many people were out on such a balmy night, most of them couples. Everyone seemed to be touching—holding hands, arms around waists or shoulders. The sound of a saxophone wafted softly from somewhere.

Emma didn't want to think that he was touching her because he had to. She wanted to believe that his hand was there because he needed to touch her, as much as she needed to be touched. Perhaps it was. Perhaps she'd been wrong about him. What if... What if he were really just a businessman who'd seen her picture in the paper? Stranger things had happened. Not to her, of course, but Ripley had made a whole career of oddities and coincidences. So why wasn't she allowed one night with a real prince?

Michael stopped her. He didn't say anything or take her arm, he just slowed and stopped, and her rhythm was his, so she paused as he did. With his free hand, he pointed out to where the Mississippi met the Gulf, to a cruise ship ablaze with lights. Floating over the black water, it was a ghost ship come from far away, and its otherworldly beauty moved her inexplicably.

"Ever been on a cruise?" Michael asked.

"No. Nothing like that."

"You should go. It's really something being out in the middle of all that water."

"Where did you go?"

"Barbados."

"Wow."

"Yeah."

"I used to dream about Barbados when I was a kid," she said. "It always seemed like a magical place."

He laughed, but it held no humor. She heard derision, cynicism, and she wondered why. It hadn't seemed an odd statement to her.

"I didn't know there was an island called Barbados when I was a kid. And I certainly didn't know about magic."

"Where are you from?"

"California. East Los Angeles."

"I've never been there, either. I'd love to go, though."

"Not to East L.A. you don't."

"Why?"

"It's a ghetto. A barrio to be more exact. You wouldn't want to get a flat tire out there."

They walked a few steps forward, until they reached the high metal barrier that separated the sidewalk from the shoreline. Michael took his hand away and leaned forward, resting on his elbows. Her back felt chilled, and she thought briefly of encouraging him to walk some more on the chance that he'd touch her again. Instead, she leaned forward too, mimicking his stance.

"Tell me," she said. "Tell me about when you lived in the barrio."

He didn't speak for a long while. Just stared at the slow moving ship. Finally, he turned to look at her. "You don't want to know," he said. "There was nothing pretty about it."

"That's all right. I don't need pretty."

She could see his frown in the moonlight. "It wasn't much. A typically dysfunctional family. Gangster friends, bad schools. The whole nine yards."

"But look at you now."

"Yeah. I've scraped my childhood off my shoes, all right."

"But?"

The saxophone grew louder for a moment, as if a door had opened letting the sound escape. Then it grew quiet again, and melancholy.

Michael stood up sharply. He coughed, and looked around, checking, she thought, for witnesses to his moment of indiscretion. "The carriages are just down the road," he said. "Let's see if we can get one."

He led her down the street toward some wonderful old Spanish buildings, and a small square with several horse-driven carriages waiting at the curb. He didn't touch her again, and she felt that whatever magic had been swirling between them had left with her question. And darn it, she wanted it back.

There were a lot more people by the carriages. A

lot more women to stare at Michael. She couldn't blame them. He was an extraordinarily handsome man. He held himself tall and straight, with a confidence that was palpable. Why would a man like him need to make a living as a paid escort? Maybe she had been wrong.

"There's one. It looks like a nice horse, doesn't it?" He pointed to a bay mare pulling a black carriage. The driver was an old man with sparse white hair, combed to perfection over a big bald patch.

"Very nice," she said.

They approached the calash and the old gentleman gave them a big, semitoothless grin. "Come on up, folks. Thirty minutes for fifteen dollars."

Michael held Emma's hand as she climbed into the black carriage. She sat on the small leather seat, amazed at how tiny the space was. She would be right up against Michael. Touching. Oh, my.

She expected him to follow, but instead, he walked to the front of the buggy. He reached into his pocket and took out a bill, she couldn't see the denomination, and held it out for the driver. They spoke briefly, but she couldn't hear the exchange. The old man nodded, smiling broadly once more, and then Michael climbed in beside her.

She had been correct in her assessment of the size of the seat. His whole left side pressed against her right side from shoulders to knees.

Before she could acclimatize to this intimacy, the carriage jolted, and she jerked forward. Michael's arm went out to stop her, landing squarely across her chest. His hand, positioned to protect her from a nasty carriage accident, lay on her breast.

Then the ride smoothed, and he withdrew, leaving her breathless. It wasn't on purpose, she assured herself. He was being gallant, trying to save her from hitting her head. But she was reminded of the time Alex Trent, her high school boyfriend, had used the same maneuver in his father's Chrysler, claiming the brakes weren't to be trusted. She'd stopped Alex posthaste, but she certainly wouldn't cry foul tonight if the horse came to a jarring halt.

Michael looked at her, a bit flustered at what he'd done.

She smiled. "Was it good for you?"

Then he laughed. It was a good laugh. Strong. Low. Sexy as hell. "Very good."

"Glad to oblige."

His brow shot up.

"Once."

His grin melted the last of her willpower. Keeping her composure was a Herculean task, but she managed. It wasn't a good idea to let the gentleman know she wasn't thinking like a lady.

"The architecture is wonderful here, isn't it?"

She looked up, surprised that they were so far away from the square. "Where are we?"

"Headed someplace very special."

"I thought this carriage went to Jackson Square?"

"Not tonight."

She turned a bit so she was facing him. "Are you kidnapping me?"

"For an hour or two."

"Should I be worried?"

"Only about sudden stops."

It was her turn to laugh. It felt easy and right to laugh at Michael's jokes. To lean back and rest her head on the leather cushion. She was surprisingly comfortable with the feel of him so close. Enchanted by the *clop-clop* of the horse's hooves on cobblestone. Bewitched by the scent of jasmine and the soft silk of the sultry air. She decided right then that she wouldn't wonder any more about why Michael was here. She would just enjoy the fact that he was.

They rode along quietly for a long stretch. Emma looked at the old buildings, knowing she should be impressed and enthralled, but all she could think of was Michael. It was her night. The prize of prizes. So what if she would wake tomorrow in her old skin, with her old job, and her old house and her old problems. Tonight she was Cinderella, Princess Jasmine, Sleeping Beauty all rolled into one.

Michael looked at the smile that played on Emma's lips. She was having a good time, he thought. So was he, which was more to the point. Why hadn't he asked her more questions about Transco? She showed no hesitance in discussing the company, so what was he waiting for?

Something else was going on. With him, not her. It seemed very important to show Emma a good time.

Not an ordinary good time, but something unique, special. He wanted her to open her eyes wide with wonder. To see things she'd never seen before. What he didn't know was why.

Was this woman so different from any other? He'd gone out with models, actresses, legendary beauties. Emma couldn't begin to compete. He dealt regularly with female executives who were smart, savvy, elegant. Emma was more down-to-earth. There was just something about her. Maybe the ease with which she smiled. Or the gentleness of her voice. Perhaps it was her clear green eyes that seemed to hold no secrets.

Whatever it was, he'd better get over it. His window of opportunity was closing. By the end of the night, he needed to get all his questions answered.

He turned, prepared to broach the subject once more. Only Emma had captured a leaf from an overhanging tree, and was brushing it softly against the skin of her cheek. It was impossible to think of anything else. His questions flew away on the breeze as he watched her. She closed her eyes, smelled the leaf, smiled her Mona Lisa smile.

He became acutely aware of his body—the lower regions to be exact. Maybe he wouldn't go home tomorrow. What was one more day?

Emma focused on her surroundings, and seemed surprised to see they had entered a business district. The streets were bare and the buildings large and utilitarian. The beautiful architecture was saved for less industrious sections of town, but hidden inside one huge warehouse was a treasure. Michael silently urged the horse on. He wanted to get there, to stand up, to cool down. Being this close to Emma wasn't good for his blood pressure.

She'd grown puzzled. "This is the special place?"

"Just wait."

"Well, if you meant to confuse me, congratulations."

"Confusion wasn't the goal."

"What was?"

"Surprise."

At last he saw it. The warehouse was lit up, just as he'd requested in his phone call. A security guard stood outside the door. The carriage stopped.

"Mr. Craig?" The guard didn't really wait for an answer. He just turned and opened the door, then flipped on a bank of light switches. Michael was afraid his surprise would be spoiled, but they couldn't see anything from outside.

He climbed down, then held Emma's hand as she descended. He led her toward the entrance, then moved behind her. "Okay, this is it."

"What?"

He moved his right hand over her eyes. "Patience. Two more seconds." He walked forward, steering her toward the door. His body pressed against her back, feeling the curves of her slight figure.

Once she was inside, and the security guard had stepped out, Michael took his hand away.

Emma's gasp told him he'd scored big time.

"My God, what is all this?"

He looked at her, unable to quit smiling at his victory. "This is where all the Mardi Gras floats live when they're not in the parade."

He couldn't take his eyes off her. She was like a child, filled with wonder as she wandered among the huge papier-mâché figures. She touched the grapes on the Bacchus float, the intricate detail on a pirate ship. There were over a dozen floats in the huge room, each one capable of holding ten or twenty riders. Emma seemed tiny and delicate next to the monstrous cartoon figures.

Michael had been here once before, but the magic of the place hadn't lived until Emma walked inside. It was just as he'd hoped. He'd given her a gift, a rare treat, and he felt like Santa Claus on Christmas morning.

"This is unbelievable," she said, her voice echoing off the concrete walls. "I've never seen anything like it."

"I'm glad."

"How did you do this?"

"The man in charge is a buddy of mine. I called him from the restaurant."

She turned to him, the same astonishment she'd had for the floats now focused on him. "You planned this back in the restaurant?"

He nodded.

"But you didn't know me."

"Sure I did. You're the Employee of the Year. It's your special night."

She let her gaze wander slowly over the room, briefly scanning each individual float. Then she turned to him, walked close and went up on her toes. She kissed his cheek. "Thank you."

"No, thank you."

"What for?"

"I'm not sure."

She flushed a bit, her soft skin infused with a shade of pink he'd never seen before. He wanted to kiss her. Not the tiny peck she'd given him, but a real kiss. A world record kiss. It could be incredible. Or it could be a big mistake.

Emma felt as though nothing in her life would ever be the same. Her heart pumped loudly in her chest, and she wondered if Michael could hear the steady beat. She touched the painted shell of a Cupid pointing his arrow into the air. Tonight, she believed in Cupid. In Donner and Blizten, too. The Tooth Fairy was real, so were the Easter Bunny and Tinkerbell. She felt like Alice in Wonderland, except she had Michael as her guide.

How could this be happening to her? Although she hadn't tried it, she was quite certain that if she looked up the word *ordinary* in the dictionary, she would find her picture. And tonight was decidedly extraordinary.

She turned to Michael, shocked once more by the

look on his face. He was watching her. Just watching. Wearing a comfortable, appreciative smile.

"Why did you bring me here?" she asked.

"Don't you like it?"

"Of course. It's fabulous. I've never seen anything like it before."

"That's why."

She moved closer to him, really studying his expression, trying to find the answer he wasn't giving her. She reached with her hand, and touched his smile with her fingertips, expecting him to vanish like all her other dreams. But he was flesh and blood. A real live man, and she was awake, alive and she was suddenly very afraid that he was exactly who he said he was.

He took her hand in his, and brought her palm to his mouth. He kissed her once, sweetly, and she could feel the softness of his lips and the heat of his breath. His gaze caught hers in an unwavering stare. She froze, frightened, excited, and felt her own heat surge inside.

He moved her hand down, slowly, never blinking or looking away. He leaned forward, and she knew he was going to kiss her. She'd never wanted anything more than that kiss. Her eyes began to close.

But the kiss didn't come. Michael stopped just shy of her lips. He moved back sharply, looked away, and dropped her hand. "I'm sorry," he said. "I didn't mean to..."

"That's all right," she said, trying not to make too much of his change of heart.

"No. We barely know each other. I didn't mean to presume."

"You don't need to worry about that," she said. "Honest. I don't think the regular rules apply tonight. How can they, with the god of wine as a chaperone?"

"You may have a point. But I have a feeling even old Bacchus would want us to take things a little slower."

She flushed, amazed at her boldness, a bit embarrassed by it, too. "Of course." She turned away from him, unsure what to do or say. This was a first for her. She'd been with other men, well, two men. She hadn't felt this awkward with either of them. It was Michael that had her flummoxed. His beautiful suit, his rich, thick hair, those hazel eyes...and who could know what to do with those lips? It was all too much.

"Hey," he said, catching her hand. He waited until she faced him. "I said we'd take it slower. Not that we wouldn't take it at all."

If she were smart, she'd pull her hand away. Ask to go back to the hotel. Thank the man for a nice evening, and leave it at that. Then she would have her memories and a little bit of mystery to play with. The what-ifs would keep her happy for a long time.

On the other hand, if she played this out, there was a very real chance that it would end badly. That she would fall too hard, and the fall would break her heart. If she were smart, she'd run for her life.

But what had smart gotten her up to now? A stable job, responsibility for her whole family, nights filled with loneliness? Just once she'd like to throw caution to the wind and let the sparks fly.

Just once...

Just tonight.

3

MICHAEL WANTED Emma back in his arms. He wanted to kiss her more than he could have ever anticipated. She wanted the same thing, he could tell from her eyes, her disappointment when he'd backed away. But was it smart? Would it get him what he needed? Very probably. So why the hesitation?

It was the look in her eyes, of course. The innocence. The hope. The pure and simple sensuality that swirled just beneath the surface. He'd known from the beginning that he was going to hurt this woman. What hadn't occurred to him was that he might care.

Caring wasn't something that happened to him often. He thought about the gift his last girlfriend had given him. His briefcase. She'd had initials engraved in gold script. RB. Ruthless Bastard. He loved that briefcase.

So why was he acting the gentleman now? He could have Emma. Tonight. It wouldn't be a hardship, either. It didn't take a genius to see that she would be a wonderful lover, and that giving her pleasure would be an experience he'd not soon forget. Of all the times to get a conscience.

"What are you thinking?" she asked.

He realized he'd been staring for a long time. "That you're very beautiful," he said, startled, because it was true.

"I'm not, but thank you."

"What's this? Surely you can't mean you don't think you're pretty?"

She withdrew her hand from his. "Don't think I'm being rude, but if it's all the same to you, I'd rather not go there."

She turned from him, eyes lowered, and started walking toward the back of the warehouse.

Michael frowned. Clearly Emma was uncomfortable with her looks, which was a shame. He was accustomed to women who were secure in their beauty, who used their looks as a tool to get what they wanted. Admittedly, Emma wasn't in the Elle Macpherson category, but she was still a very attractive woman. It wasn't right that she didn't know it.

He followed Emma, watching her from the back. Her posture was so straight that his earlier notion that she'd been a dancer was reconfirmed. Only ballerinas walked with that funny little gait, and held themselves so tall. He'd like to see her dance. With that poetic soul of hers, she'd be good.

Poetic soul? What was he getting into here? He had some very specific questions he needed answers to, nothing more. As soon as he'd seen her picture in the paper, he'd realized the way to get those answers. He hadn't actually planned to take her to bed, nothing so concrete, but he wouldn't hesitate if that was his only option. After all, he was a ruthless bastard, wasn't he? So what was the problem? And why was he so concerned with **the** nature of Emma's soul?

She turned then, and he saw the hint of sadness on her face. Instead of the awed smile of just a few moments ago, her lips turned down in a slight frown. Her eyes seemed troubled, and the pink flush had left her cheeks.

He kept on walking until he was close enough to touch her. They stood directly beneath a huge pirate ship. Emma looked up at him, then her gaze lowered.

"Maybe we should go," she said, so softly he barely heard her.

"We can, but you haven't seen everything yet."

"That's okay. It's late."

"It's only late in the real world, Emma. Here, it's early."

Her gaze lifted, and met his. "I keep trying to keep the real world away. It has a nasty habit of not letting me."

"You don't have enough practice, that's all. But I do. And I'm a hell of a teacher."

She didn't respond. Instead, she studied his face unabashedly. Really examined him. From his forehead, slowly to his eyes, his nose, his mouth. It was hard not to look away. He wasn't used to such scrutiny. Most people were too intimidated to look him in the eye, let alone take the time to explore his face in detail.

"You aren't from an escort service, are you?"

"What?"

"My friends didn't hire you, did they?"

"I'm sorry, I don't know what you're talking about."

She nodded. "You're too handsome, for one thing. But more than that, you're too confident."

"Did I miss something?"

She smiled at him. "No. I did."

"Care to explain?"

She shook her head. Then she leaned forward, and slowly, very slowly, brought her lips to his. The kiss was so gentle, it was barely there at all. Just a whisper. But it still managed to knock him for a loop.

"What was that for?" he asked.

"That was for saying I was beautiful," she said, then she did it again. This time, the kiss was a bit more substantial.

"And that?" he murmured.

"Because you brought me here."

Once again, she leaned forward. This time, her lips lingered a moment, then two, before she broke it off. "That one was for joining me for dinner."

"I—"

She didn't let him finish. She closed her eyes and kissed him once more, but now there were no whispers. No delicate pressure from a poet. This time, she kissed him with a whole different kind of message. One he understood immediately.

His arms went around her back instinctively, pulling her close. The feel of her body pressed against his stirred him, and he wanted, no needed, to taste her fully. He parted his lips, and met no resistance. She was sweet and warm and moist, and her tongue explored his with matching intensity. He felt her arms go around his neck, and her head shifted a bit to the left, which made a perfect fit. He felt her muscles relax, her mouth become bolder. Then, she pulled back. She broke the kiss before he was ready, and he tried to hold her close, but her hands went to his chest and he let her go.

"What was that one for?" he asked, surprised at how low and gruff his voice sounded.

"That was because I wanted to," she said. "Now, I think we'd better go back."

He thought for a moment that she was asking him to take her back so they could pick up where she'd left off. But looking into her eyes, he knew that wasn't going to happen. She meant for him to take her back, and say goodbye.

"Are you sure?" he asked, reaching out with his hand to stroke her soft cheek.

She let him, but it didn't melt her resolve. "I'm sure."

"May I ask why?"

Her lips curled into a tiny smile. "No."

"May I guess?"

"If you want to."

"I think you're afraid, Emma. Afraid that I won't turn out to be a prince."

The color returned to her cheeks. He imagined that she would have that glow when they made love.

"I won't deny it," she said.

"You're right, of course. I'm no prince. I'm just a man." He moved his hand behind her head, and very gently pulled her closer. He kissed her then, still gentle. But she didn't have to tell him to stop. He was the one to pull back.

"What was that for?" she whispered.

"That was because I didn't expect you. Because I didn't expect this."

"I don't understand."

"I thought you'd be a diversion. Not a problem."

"A problem?" She stepped back a bit, just out of his reach, a smile playing about her lips. "I think I like that."

"Oh, really?"

She nodded. "I've never been anyone's problem before. Although I'm not so thrilled with being a diversion."

"We passed diversion way back at the restaurant."

She leaned against the pirate ship, and her dress pulled against her body. Her curves illustrated his point. She was a problem. He wasn't lying. He wanted her. Tonight. Now. But he wanted her in a way that put him at a disadvantage. That couldn't happen. "Come on," he said. "You're right. We should go back."

A flicker of disappointment crossed her face, but the smile didn't waver. "Right. Back to the real world."

He nodded, a little sadly. If things had been different, he would have liked to explore this world with her. Perhaps take her up into this pirate ship. Make love to her right under the eyes of Bacchus. But things weren't different. She was a means to an end. If he let his feelings get in the way, he could kiss Transco goodbye.

She walked next to him, taking one final look at all the floats as they headed for the door. Just before they went outside, she stopped, kissed his cheek, and said, "Thank you. It was the best present I've ever had."

That bothered him for the rest of the night.

EMMA AWOKE reluctantly. Her dreams had been filled with pirate ships and smiling gods. And Michael. He'd been almost as wonderful in her sleep as he had been in person. In some ways, better. No, she'd been better. She'd known what to say, how to act. She'd been as comfortable with Michael as she was with her business associates, and once her discomfort was gone, it had been easy to hear him say she was beautiful. That part of the dream stuck with her even after she got out of bed. The feeling of pleasure, instead of disbelief.

What was he doing right now? She turned on the shower and slipped off her nightgown. Was he awake? It was only seven. Of course he would be, she decided. A man like him wouldn't need much sleep. Perhaps, like her, he was climbing into the shower. Naked. Oh, my.

The warm water felt wonderful, and it was just the right pressure, too. Her shower at home was skimpy at best. She always felt as if she needed to run around in a circle to get wet. But this...this was luxury. She lathered up the washcloth and closed her eyes, letting herself enjoy the sensual feel of the rich soap on her skin. In a second, her thoughts turned once more to Michael, and they were definitely not G-rated.

She remembered his kiss, the taste of him as sharp and clear as if only a moment had passed, not a whole night. If only she could hold on to the memory, keep it this vivid. But that wouldn't happen. In time it would fade, become distant. More like something read in a book. Oh well. She could conjure it up now in exquisite detail. That would have to do.

Just to be a little daring she used the hotel shampoo instead of what she'd brought from home. It smelled delicious. When was the last time she'd changed shampoos? Or makeup? Or experimented with her hairstyle? Never, that's when.

She'd become an old woman. Not chronologically, but in her way of thinking. The girls had told her, but she hadn't listened. Of course, they had been a little obtuse. When Christie mentioned that Emma's makeup reminded her of a Seurat painting, it hadn't occurred to Emma that she meant it was a hundred years out of date.

When she got home, she was going to go for that makeover, dammit. Not because of Michael. Well, not just because of Michael. But because she'd had a taste of what it might be like to feel good about her looks, not just her research abilities. So what if there was no place in her life to meet men. She had to look at herself in the mirror every day, didn't she? Wasn't she worth feeling pretty?

She rinsed her hair, put on some conditioner, and for once, didn't even mind shaving her legs. Instead of the awful chore it usually was, she toyed with the idea of Michael touching her thigh. Her smooth thigh. She didn't nick herself, even once.

By the time she'd rinsed, stepped out of the shower, wrapped herself in the big fluffy hotel towel and gone to the closet to pick out something to wear, she'd decided that Michael or no Michael, she was going to have a magnificent day. A day so full of adventure, she'd never forget it.

MICHAEL WAS IN AND OUT of the shower in two minutes. While he shaved, he concentrated on nothing else. Just the razor. At least, that was his intention. But Emma intruded again.

He'd had a bad night. Which wasn't at all like him. He'd trained himself to get to sleep fast and hard.

That's why he didn't need as much sleep as other people. Four or five hours kept him feeling rested and healthy. It was simply a matter of turning his mind off. His secretary liked to call it a beta state of meditation, but he knew it was simply a matter of discipline. It didn't matter where he was, on an airplane, in a strange house, or even sitting up in some train station, he could be out in a flash. Except for last night.

Emma kept popping into his thoughts. Each time he forced her out, she came in another way. Sometimes it was her image. Another time, it was the sound of her voice, or the smell of her skin. She just wouldn't leave him alone.

By five-thirty, he'd figured out what he needed to do. Get his information, and get the hell out of Dodge. Get as far away from Emma and her distractions as he could.

He rinsed his face, then went back into his room to dress. Since he didn't know her well, he had no idea if she slept late or was an early riser. At first he'd assumed she'd sleep in; this was her vacation after all. But the more he thought about it, the more he was convinced she'd get up at her workweek hour. In either case, he was going to be in the lobby when she came down.

So it was settled. He put on his jeans and his Polo shirt, his shoes and socks, combed his hair, checked to make sure he had enough cash.

And thought about Emma.

WHERE THE HELL WAS SHE? Michael folded the newspaper he'd been trying to read for the last hour, and stood up. It was hard to maintain his nonchalance. He wanted her to think he just happened to be downstairs, just happened to be reading the paper, when she got off the elevator. But it was already seven, and no Emma. Maybe he should just call her, and invite her to breakfast. No, he'd already decided this was the plan, and he didn't like to deviate, even if it was inconvenient. He'd thought this through. She needed to be totally convinced that he had nothing on his mind but a relaxing day.

By the time he started asking her about Transco, she needed to be completely at ease. Not that he was going to ask her anything proprietary. He was more concerned with Phil Bailey and what he wanted. Emma would know. If he played his cards right, she would give him the formula that would convince Bailey to sell. Maybe he wanted to move to Hawaii. Or maybe he wanted to continue to be part of the research and development team. Michael had a feeling Bailey's biggest concern was his environmental work. Which could be dealt with. But Michael needed to know what Bailey's Achilles' heel was, and Emma was going to tell him. If she ever came down from her room.

He walked over to the gift shop window. From his position he could see the elevator doors, and he wouldn't look so damn conspicuous. Twice now, he'd gotten strange looks from bellmen.

The elevator dinged, and he held his breath. Emma walked out.

He turned, casually, and walked toward her. He didn't look at her again until he heard her say, "Michael!" Then he looked up.

Her smile knocked him out. She seemed so damn glad to see him. Her face lit up, her eyes shimmered. He couldn't help but smile back.

"What are you doing here?" she asked. "I thought you had to go back to Houston."

"I changed my plans."

"Oh? Did Bubba decide he liked the opera after all?"

Michael smiled briefly, then grew serious. "No. I stayed because of you, Emma."

Her easy grin froze, and her eyes widened. Lovely green eyes. Her hair was down again, too, which pleased him. Her jeans were faded, but fashionably so. They looked awfully good on her, as did the crisp blue blouse. Dammit, what was it about her that had him thinking like this?

"You don't mean it," Emma said. He could hear the hope in her voice.

"I certainly do. You, Miss Roberts, need a tour guide. I would like to apply for the position."

"You're hired," she said. Then she blushed.

He saw it start at her delicate neck and spread upward to infuse her cheeks with pink. It was going to be a good day. He took her hand in his, and marveled again at her soft fragility. "Come on, Cinderella," he said. "Let's go find ourselves a pumpkin."

"Where are we going?" she asked, as he led her toward the street.

"Café du Monde of course. No trip to the Big Easy would be complete without beignets and café au lait."

"I've always wanted to go there."

"You let me know what you've always wanted, Emma, and I'll make sure you have it."

She gave him a funny grin, but didn't say anything more. He held the door open for her, and then followed her outside. Of course, his gaze moved south. Yep, those jeans looked mighty good.

They passed on taking a carriage, and ended up walking the dozen blocks to the open-air café at the French Market. The lines were long, but that didn't bother Michael. He really was enjoying himself. The conversation was easy and light. She was excited about visiting this landmark, and he saw it through her eyes. With its tall pillars and green-and-white striped awning, its shiny black ceiling fans whirring above the sea of tables and chairs, it was to him the very essence of New Orleans.

Full of delicious smells, laughing people, street musicians just a step or two away, it made him feel at home, even though he visited rarely. Seeing Emma's delight made it all the sweeter.

Emma. Just like last night, he found her funny and smart. It turned out to be easy to bring up Transco and Phil Bailey, and by the time they'd found a table and were sipping the chicory coffee and eating the messy but delicious donuts, he had most of the information he needed. It was like shooting ducks in a barrel. Emma was open and honest, concerned about her boss, grateful, he thought, to be able to discuss her work with someone so sympathetic.

Another twenty minutes, and he knew how to strike, when to act, and what his bargaining chips were. Emma had given him all the ammunition he could have hoped for.

He excused himself for a moment and found a telephone. All during his conversation he kept thinking of Emma back at the table. When she found out, she was going to be devastated. She'd hate his guts. And he wouldn't blame her. The kindest thing he could do right now was leave. Tell her some emergency had come up, and he had to get back to Houston immediately.

But he couldn't. He finished the call and went back to her. For a long while he just sat there, listening to her talk and laugh. He wanted to spend the day with her. He wanted to show her New Orleans. He wanted to kiss her again.

"So what's next?" she asked, cocking her head slightly to the left.

He had to make up his mind. Now. Then he noticed she had a little speck of powdered sugar at the very edge of her mouth. He leaned forward and kissed that spot, tasting her sweetness. Then he leaned back to look in her eyes. Her pleasure gave him his answer. "This town is filled with magic, Emma. Let me show it to you."

4

EMMA RELAXED into Michael's arms. It was the best place she'd ever been, and she quietly sent pleas to whoever was in charge of street entertainers that the cellist on the corner would never stop playing. She knew the music, recognized the melancholy notes, but she couldn't recall the name of the piece. It didn't matter. Nothing mattered, except that she was here, Michael had his arm around her shoulder, and her head rested on his chest.

His scent filled her senses, forcing her to close her eyes. Indefinable, except for the hint of soap, the scent branded itself in her memory. Intoxicating, that's what he smelled like. Male and clean and rich and deep.

The morning had been ripe with new experiences. The city alone would have captivated her, but with Michael as her guide, each sight was even more special. Jackson Square, the French Quarter, the incredible hotels and quaint restaurants. The weekend would never be sufficient to see it all. On the other hand, she would be just as content to sit down in a back booth at Denny's for the rest of her stay, as long as Michael was there with her.

Her suspicions about him had vanished. He wasn't a paid escort, that much she'd determined when they'd talked this morning over coffee. His knowledge of the business world was born of experience. He knew a lot about oil exploration, which somehow didn't surprise her. It occurred to her that she still didn't know exactly what he did. She sighed. Maybe she'd ask. Later.

Right now, she had to concentrate on the way his hand, resting on her shoulder, rubbed back and forth, very gently.

"You about ready for the next stop?"

She looked up, seeing only his chin. Although she hated to move, she leaned back far enough so she could see his face. His smile did peculiar things to her stomach. Peculiar, nice things. "Sure," she said.

"Don't you want to know what the next stop is?"

She nodded, but there was no conviction in it.

He laughed. "Emma, what am I going to do with you?"

"Whatever you want," she said. Then she realized what she'd said and she winced. "Wait, that's not what it sounded like."

He shifted so that his other hand grasped her right shoulder, and he was looking at her straight on. "No?"

With those eyes staring at her, she couldn't lie. "Well..."

"That poses an interesting dilemma."

"It does?"

He nodded. "There are any number of things I'd like to do with you, Ms. Roberts."

"Oh, heavens."

"And then some."

She blinked, and then his lips turned up in a beguiling grin.

"Why do I feel like I've just stepped smack into the center of your web?" she asked.

"Hmmm. A spider, eh? Eight arms?"

"Legs, Michael. Legs."

"Oh, yeah. Forget it, then."

It was her turn to laugh. "Okay, so what is the next stop?"

He waggled his eyebrows. "Come with me."

Of course, she did. When his palm slipped over hers, she grasped it easily, as if their hands had always been meant to fit. Just walking down the street made her incredibly happy. One thing she noticed was how many people looked at them. Not just idle glances, but real looks, sometimes stares. The women were probably noticing how incredibly handsome Michael was, which made sense to her. But the men? Perhaps they were staring at Michael, too. New Orleans was a sophisticated city. The idea made her smile.

They turned corner after corner, going toward the outskirts of the Quarter. She was completely lost, but Michael seemed to know just which side street to take. The shops they passed all looked interesting to her, especially the costume shops and the little independent bookstores.

"Here we are."

She looked at the window display in front of her. There wasn't much there to clue her in to the type of shop it was, just a few books, and some New Age type crystals and such. Then she noticed the small wooden sign above the door. A voodoo shop! "You're kidding!"

Michael shook his head. "Nope. It's the real Mc-Coy."

"I've read about this stuff. About the plant extract in Haiti that paralyzes the victim so they appear dead, even when they're not. The doctors miss the faint heartbeat and bury the person, and when they come out of the stupor, they claw their way out of the grave. The real walking dead." She grabbed Michael around the neck and gave him a fierce hug. "This is so cool!"

"I had no idea you were going to like it this much," he said, grinning. "Maybe I shouldn't have brought you here. It might give you ideas."

She grinned right back. "Yeah. You'd better watch your step. I don't think you'd like being a zombie. They never get the best tables."

He wrapped his arms around her waist and brought her close. His laughter rumbled in his chest and she felt it all the way through her. Then he kissed her, long, slow and deep, and she knew right then that Michael Craig could have his way with her.

MICHAEL WATCHED EMMA. He watched as she crooked her head to the side to read the titles of the books in the cramped store. Funny how he'd known she'd like this place. He'd first been here three years ago, just for a few moments, at the request of his date. At the time, he'd thought the whole thing was silly, but now, through Emma's eyes, he saw the appeal. She was so eager to learn everything. To explore and feel and taste. He remembered a movie he'd seen once called *Awakenings*, with Robert De Niro and Robin Williams, in which De Niro awakened from a long state of disease-induced catatonia. How the character had seen life with a child's eye, a stranger's curiosity. That was how Emma looked at the potions and the books and the trinkets.

All he could think of was having that eager curiosity and excitement focused on him. In bed. Making love to Emma promised to be an experience he'd not soon forget. He had a distinct feeling she wasn't experienced. Not a virgin, he was pretty sure of that, but a novice. But oh, what a student she'd be. And how he wanted to be her teacher.

His conscience hadn't left him completely alone, although ever since he'd kissed the sugar from her lips this morning, there was really no choice in the matter. Emma would be his, and all he could hope for was that after it was all over, and she'd had a chance to see what he could do for the company, she'd forgive him and look back at today with affection. Hell, she was having a great time, she couldn't deny that. And things were only going to get better.

The hard part was holding back. Not jumping into a cab right now and racing to the hotel. He'd been in a constant state of arousal all day. Not the kind of arousal that had made him walk with his books in front of his lap back in junior high, but close. This was a little more subtle, and twice as maddening.

"Here," Emma said, holding out a little rag doll in one hand, a half dozen long hat pins in the other.

"What's this?" he asked, taking the voodoo doll from her.

"A present."

"Who's the victim?"

"I can't say for you, but I have quite a little list of folks who are suddenly going to get neck aches next week."

"Emma, I'm shocked."

She lifted her left brow. "Why?"

"You're so... I can't imagine you having any enemies."

"Sweet. You were going to say sweet, weren't you?"

"Yeah, I suppose I was."

"See that? If I didn't like you so much, that would have deserved a pin. Well, maybe not a pin. A little pinch."

"Why? What's wrong with being sweet?"

She sighed. "Nothing, I suppose. Unless that's all people see. I can be sweet, but that's not really me.

I'm a lot of other things, too. It's like being patted on the head."

"I see," he said. He did, too. Now that he thought about it, the term could be dismissive. "So, what would you like people to call you?"

"Ms. Roberts."

He smiled. "No, I mean an adjective. What would you like them to think about you?"

She was quiet for a moment. Staring at him, but not seeing him. "Funny," she said, her voice a lot quieter. "My first thought was that I wanted people to think I was smart. Then I changed my mind. But, now, no. I think I do want people to think I'm smart."

"Why not both?"

"Hm?"

"I said why not both? Smart *and* beautiful."

She blushed, confirming his guess. Now her gaze went down to the floor. "How did you know?"

"Because that's how I see you. Smart and beautiful. And sweet. So don't worry, Ms. Roberts. People aren't so narrow. Some are even pretty intuitive."

Emma reached up and touched him lightly on the cheek. Her wide eyes asked the question before she spoke. "Where in the world did you come from?"

He couldn't answer her. Instead, he pulled her tight to him, and kissed her. His arousal was no longer subtle.

SOMEHOW, THEY GOT BACK to the hotel. Emma wasn't sure how. They'd walked, but the streets had blended together. It could have been five blocks or fifty.

All she knew was that she was alone with the most exciting man she'd ever met, in his suite, sipping cognac, preparing to do something she'd never dreamed in a million years she would ever do. She was going to make love. To a man she barely knew. And she was going to relish every moment of it.

"Should I pour you another drink?" Michael asked as he walked to the couch with the bottle.

She shook her head. "No, thanks. I'm pretty tipsy now."

He crooked his brow. "Already?"

She nodded. "I'm not much of a drinker. Especially when it's the hard stuff."

He put the bottle on the coffee table and sat down next to her. Right next to her. Just like in the carriage ride last night, their bodies touching from shoulder to thigh. And just like last night, it took her breath away.

Michael stared at her, a small inscrutable smile on his lips. "Your face is wonderful," he said.

She felt her cheeks warm and she glanced away, but his fingers on her chin gently moved her head back until she was looking at him once more.

"Don't be embarrassed," he said, his voice so kind she knew he was speaking honestly. "I mean it. You're not hard to read, Ms. Roberts. Your eyes tell so much about you."

"What do they say now?" she asked, surprised at how bold and excited she felt.

He didn't answer for a moment. Then he leaned toward her, putting his lips gently on hers. He kissed her very lightly, then released the pressure, but he didn't pull away. Instead, he whispered, "They say yes." He moved that brief distance again, but this time, his kiss was anything but gentle.

She fell into his embrace, thrilled at his passion. Her body seemed electrified, as if his lips and hers together created something entirely new, alive, sizzling. She opened her mouth and when she tasted him, the sizzle skittered all the way through her.

This was so new, this kind of wanting. No one had told her it could be like this. She'd read about it, but always with an air of skepticism. Now she knew the fireworks they talked about were real.

He shifted on the couch, sliding his arm behind her, pulling her closer. Her hands cupped his face as she explored his taste and scent and feel. How had she gotten so lucky? She must have saved an orphanage in a past life or something. Nothing else could explain what she was doing in his arms.

She opened her eyes. To her surprise, his were open, too. He pulled slightly back, breaking the kiss. He swallowed, never moving his gaze from hers. "We can stop now, if you want," he said, his voice husky and low. "Because in another minute, I don't know if I'll be able to."

Taking in a deep breath, Emma moved her left

hand from his cheek and lowered it very slowly to his thigh. His gaze followed. She screwed up her courage and shifted her hand up and to the right. He clearly hadn't been kidding about his doubts. She felt him, thick and hard beneath her fingers. Moaning, he brought his hand to hers and pressed down as his gaze moved back up. "Are you sure?"

She nodded. "More than I've ever been about anything."

"Remember, Emma. I'm not a prince."

She closed her eyes and leaned forward. Just before her lips touched his, she whispered, "Oh, yes you are."

This time, it was her kiss. Her tongue darted into his mouth, tasting, licking. She felt a hunger so deep it could never be satisfied with just a kiss. When he broke away, she gasped. He rose to his feet, and held his arms out to her. Without a moment's hesitation, she went to him, and when he reached around and lifted her into his arms, she nearly expired from bliss.

He *was* a prince, if only for a day, and she was a princess. He carried her quickly, urgently, through the living room into his bedroom. She barely noticed the decor, except for the king-size bed. He laid her down gently, then stared at her for a long moment.

"What?" she asked, afraid that something was wrong.

"You're so beautiful."

"No," she said. "You are."

He sat down and brushed the side of her face with

the back of his hand. "Emma, what are you doing to me?"

"I don't know, but I think it's mutual."

He nodded. Then he leaned down and kissed her once on the lips. "I want you so much," he whispered. "But..."

"I want you," she said, not letting him finish. "Please."

"I can't promise you anything."

"I'm not asking for promises." She raised herself until she was on her knees next to him, never letting go of his gaze. Then she reached down and began to unbutton her blouse.

He never moved. He just watched her.

She'd never undressed like this in front of a man. Never so blatantly, with the lights on, on top of the covers. But she'd never felt this way with a man before. She wanted to do things with him she'd never dreamed of—well, that she'd never admitted she dreamed of. He was more a fantasy than a reality, and right now, she felt as if she were unreal, too. That this was a dream, a wish granted. She felt absolutely no shame, no hesitation.

The last button came undone, and she pulled her blouse off. His gaze shifted from her eyes to her breasts then back again. While he watched, she reached behind and undid the clasp of her bra. Slowly, teasing, she lowered the straps, then she took the bra away and dropped it over the side of the bed.

My God, here she was, half naked in front of him,

her nipples so tight she didn't have to look down to know they were erect. His hand came tentatively forward, almost as if he were afraid to touch her. Then she felt his palm on her right breast and she couldn't hold back her moan. She leaned forward, filling his hand.

His groan picked up where hers left off, and he moved closer to her on the bed. His other hand touched her, lightly playing over the sensitive flesh. He kissed her lips, then trailed down her cheek to her chin, to her neck, then her chest. She closed her eyes and arched her back as he reached her nipple. First, she felt his tongue, then the gentle suction of his mouth.

It was like nothing she'd ever felt before. Wanton and erotic beyond her imagination. She cupped the back of his head to keep him there, never wanting him to stop his ministrations. What was he doing to her? Such magical lips, such a talented tongue. She moaned and moved in an unconscious rhythm, pressing against him, and trying to ease the pressure between her legs.

When he broke away from her, her eyes flew open. Just in time to see him reach for the bottom of his T-shirt and pull it over his head.

She inhaled sharply at the sight of his chest. She'd only seen one other man who looked this good, and he'd been on television, so it didn't count. Michael was stunning. Broad muscled shoulders, pecs so firm she could bounce a quarter off them. Dark hair, just thick enough to make him incredibly manly without looking like a bear. His chest tapered to his slim waist and as she watched, he undid his button-fly jeans, his fingers fumbling in his haste. When he stood to finish the job, she reached for her own jeans. But she had to stop when he took his off. It was his body. It stunned her, plain and simple. He was the most gorgeous creature on the earth. Washboard stomach, firm thighs, and...oh, my.

She swallowed. Then swallowed again. His erection required a moment of silence. Maybe two or three.

He didn't let her look for long, though. Instead, he came onto the bed, and helped her finish undressing. She felt a moment of shyness, knowing she wasn't half as beautiful as he was, hoping he wouldn't be disappointed. But once she was naked, and he laid her down on her back, her worry vanished. The way he looked at her told her he was pleased. Pleased and hungry.

"Oh, Emma. I had no idea."

"What?"

"You're exquisite."

"So are you."

He shook his head. "No. You don't understand."

"Tell me."

He reached out first, and ran his hand down her stomach. She shivered at his featherlight touch. He explored her slowly, touching her skin as if it were the most delicate silk in the world. Closing her eyes, she let the sensations take over. Each time his hand moved, her flesh caught fire. She felt his reverence, his appreciation, and for the first time in her life she felt beautiful. Really beautiful. It was his touch. And the sound of his breathing. The sigh that escaped as his palm lingered on her thigh.

Then she felt his lips replace his hand.

Emma spread her legs. She did so unconsciously, easily, as if it were the most natural thing in the world to reveal her most private self to this man. She opened her eyes briefly, and watched him move on the bed so that his body was no longer at an angle, but in line with hers. His smile when he caught her looking was half wicked, half dreamy, and then she couldn't see his smile anymore. His mouth was better occupied.

She gasped at his first touch. She had never been this sensitive, this ready. He used his fingers and his lips and his tongue to send her into a spiral of desire and heat. Her hands grabbed the bedspread, and then she was able to rock slightly, matching his rhythms. It was impossible to be silent. As her breathing deepened, she moaned long and low, the fire in her belly expanding until she was engulfed in flames.

She heard another sound. It was Michael, and he, too, was moaning his pleasure. It was almost too much for her to believe. How could gratifying her give him the kind of satisfaction she heard? But she couldn't think about that now, not when she was going crazy. Not when he did that right there.

Her head thrashed on the pillow, and all the muscles in her body tightened like bowstrings. Her pelvis lifted from the bed, and Michael rose with her. He never let up, not for a second, and then she was gone. Electrical spasms coursed through her body, one after the other, and she heard her voice, so loud, yet so far away, saying his name over and over.

He released her, and she collapsed, but in another second, he moved up, so he was poised on top of her. After a moment's pause, and the sound of tearing foil, his knees pushed hers apart. He found her gaze, locked on to her, and then, in one unbelievably intense motion, he thrust into her.

The spasms continued as he filled her so completely she felt as if she'd been made whole for the first time. Looking up at him, she felt awed that his need was so clear on his face. The desire, desire for *her*, shone in his eyes.

"Emma," he whispered. "What are you doing to me? I can't...."

Her arms went to his waist and her hips bucked in a dance she didn't know she knew. Gasping for air, she wrapped her legs around him so he could enter her farther. It was more than she could stand, and the spasms started again. Rich, deep, all the way to her soul, they rocked her and sent her mind adrift so that all that existed were sensations.

"I can't hold on," he said, his voice shaking. His

jaw muscles tensed, and she could see the cords in his neck. He looked as if he were in pain, the pressure was so great, and then he filled her to the brink, and he growled an animal growl that rumbled through his chest to hers.

Finally, he relaxed. Uncurling her legs, they settled into a new position, still joined, but touching in a different way. She could feel his rapid breathing, and knew hers was just as fast. He'd wrung her out like a rag, and all that was left of her were the echoes of her climax.

"Wow," she said.

He laughed, and she felt that, too. "You can say that again."

"I had no idea."

"Hm?" He shifted a bit, and for a second she thought he was going to move away, but he didn't. He just got more comfortable.

"I mean," she said, "that I've never had that happen before."

"What?"

"You know."

"No. Tell me."

She met his gaze to see if he was teasing her. He was. She pinched him lightly.

"Hey!"

"You deserved that."

"Why won't you tell me? Surely you can't still be shy. Not after what we just did."

"I am shy. I can't help it."

He lifted himself up on one elbow and looked at her sternly. "You are many things, Emma, but you're not shy. You can't fool me." He leaned down and kissed her, then he smiled. "You, my little one, are a wild woman."

"I'm not."

"Then who did I just have my way with?"

She giggled. "All right. So sometimes I can get a little carried away."

"Ha! If we'd gone on any longer, they would have had to carry me away on a stretcher."

"I bet you say that to all the girls."

His expression changed then. He grew serious, and somehow, darker. "No. Don't you dare think that. Ever."

She nodded, a sudden tightness filling her chest. "All right. I won't."

Then, as if a switch had turned on, his humor was back. "I hate to do this. I really do. But I have to move."

She sighed dramatically. "All right. If you must."

He kissed her quickly, then he did move, and she wanted him back immediately. But that wasn't going to happen. He wasn't hers, and she'd best remember that. This was a once-in-a-lifetime experience. He'd made it something she'd never forget.

Michael went into the bathroom and closed the door. While he took care of business, he tried to get control of himself. The guilt he felt was completely out of proportion to the deed. He'd given Emma several opportunities to back out, and she hadn't. On the contrary. She'd been more than willing. What had really caught him off guard was his own reaction to making love with her.

In all the years he'd been with women, nothing like that had happened to him before. Not the act of course, but the feelings that had come with it. It wasn't like him. Sure he enjoyed sex, but there had always been a small part of himself he held back. It was only prudent. He couldn't afford to let go completely. Yet that's just what he'd done with Emma. He'd never felt more exposed, more vulnerable, than when he'd been inside her.

The hell of it was that he wanted to go right back. One time wasn't enough. He had the sinking feeling that a hundred, a thousand times, wouldn't be. But that's all he was going to get. One time.

Come Monday morning, Emma Roberts was going to hate him. Sure, it would pass eventually, but while it lasted, it wasn't going to be pretty. Yesterday, that fact hadn't bothered him. Today, it mattered a lot. Too much. And that wasn't good.

It was time to let her go. To send her off, and forget her. He was a ruthless bastard, and now he was going to prove it.

5

EMMA BLINKED AWAKE. It was her first morning back in her own bed, and for a second she felt a little disoriented. Probably because of her dreams. *Michael.* He'd lived in her head now for three days. She had gone over every moment they'd spent together, flushing with heat when she got to Saturday night. There was even the bittersweet memory of their goodbye. He'd been perfect, said the right words, kissed her so tenderly. It had been hard not to ask if she could see him again, but she hadn't. She didn't want the cold hard truth to tarnish one second of her fairy-tale weekend.

But now she was back in the real world, and it was time to take off her glass slippers and put on her sensible shoes. All she had to do was get through the day. Then she could come back home, make an excuse to go to bed early, and she could meet him once more in her dreams. He would never change. He would never disappoint her. It would always and forever be the most perfect of weekends with the most perfect of men. No one could take that away from her.

Somehow, she managed to get up. As she got

ready, she realized nothing would ever be the same again. The simple act of washing her hair was different because his hands had done the task on Sunday morning. Lathering her body with soap was now a sensual act, instead of a brisk but necessary procedure. Drying her body made her aware of every place he'd touched and kissed. He'd altered the very fabric of her world, and she'd never see him again. But it was too late for regrets now. She'd have to be satisfied with having known him once.

"YOU'RE BACK!"

Emma smiled. It was good to see her friends. They all certainly seemed glad to see her, too. You'd think she'd been gone for a year, instead of a long weekend. Christie, Margaret and Jane. Her very own Three Musketeers. The best damn research team in the business, and so much more.

They ushered her into their spacious office. Their computers were all booted up and running. Usually, Emma was the first to arrive in the morning, but today, everyone had been here to greet her.

"Tell us everything," Margaret said, ushering Emma over to the couch. "Every detail."

"Wait till you hear what's been happening here," Christie said excitedly. "You won't believe it."

"You want coffee or tea?" Jane asked as she poured herself a cup of decaf.

Emma laughed. They'd all spoken at once, and she didn't know where to start. No, wait. She did. "Coffee, thanks." She could use another cup. It promised to be an interesting morning.

She took the cup from Jane, and waited until she'd gotten comfortable before she turned to Christie. "What do you mean? What's happened?"

Christie looked from Margaret to Jane, then settled her gaze on Emma. She waited just long enough, then said, "He's selling the company."

"What?" Emma put her cup down. "Who?"

"Phil, of course. Who do you think?"

"But when?"

"It started last night."

"On a Sunday?"

Jane nodded. "I found out because he called me."

"Why?"

"He needed some numbers. That's when he told me he'd been handed an offer."

"That's it? He was handed an offer and he took it, just like that?"

Margaret nodded. That was it, then. Margaret never guessed. She knew. At forty-five, she was the eldest of the group, and like a big sister, or a mother hen, she took great care of them all. Her advice was always thoughtful, her cautions legendary, and her heart as big as Texas. She even looked the part. Large in body, and in spirit, she wore her naturally graying hair in a conservative page boy. She dressed simply, but with a sense of style that was clearly her own.

Interestingly enough, Margaret and Christie, six years her junior and anything but conservative, were as close as they could be. Perhaps it was because Christie had lost her mother so young. And it didn't hurt that Margaret encouraged Christie to be herself, which included an eclectic taste in clothing; today she wore a short black mini skirt and a man's white shirt, which somehow managed to look great on her.

Jane, on the other hand, was more Laura Ashley than Todd Oldham. Almost six feet tall, Emma always envied her sense of grace. She was a beautiful, wonderful woman, and luckily, her husband Elliott treasured her.

Now all three of her dear friends were staring at her, watching for her reaction to this stunning news. They'd been a team for so long, what would they do if the new owners decided to make a change? It was too horrible to contemplate.

"Did Phil say who made the offer?"

"A company called MRC," Jane said. "We were going to look it up this morning, but we haven't had a chance yet."

"I've never heard of it," Margaret said. "That doesn't bode well."

"Maybe they'll keep Phil on to run things," Christie suggested. "Or you could talk him out of it. He'll listen to you, Emma."

Emma shook her head. She'd known for a long while that Phil wanted out. Africa and his safaris called to him. His photography had been his primary interest since she'd known him. This was just what he had been waiting for. However, she knew he cared a great deal about the company, and his employees. Surely he would see to it that everyone was provided for. "I'll go talk to him," she said, "but I doubt I can make him change his mind."

"You can't go yet," Jane said. "You didn't tell us about this weekend."

She felt an unbidden smile, completely uncalled for given the topic of conversation, spread over her face. Just the thought of Michael, and her special time with him, turned on the glow inside her.

"Wow," Christie said. "You aren't going anywhere till you explain that."

"I'll say," Jane piped in. "I need a fresh cup of coffee for this, I can tell."

Emma felt her cheeks warm. She'd toyed with the idea of keeping the weekend and Michael to herself. But that wasn't likely. These women were her best friends. They could read her like a book. Whether she wanted to tell them or not, they'd get it out of her. Of course, she wouldn't tell them *everything*.

"Go on," Margaret said, leaning forward in the big club chair. "We don't have all day."

Emma smiled again. "I met someone."

Her three cohorts exchanged surprised looks.

"Hey, it's possible."

"Of course it is. You're gorgeous and funny and brilliant." Jane gave her a playful swat on the leg. "You're the one who's been going for the world celibacy record. Which, I hope, is now out of the question."

"Jane!" Emma blushed fiercely.

Jane leaned back. "Thank God. Now, details."

"Just for that, I shouldn't tell you anything."

"But you will."

Emma sighed. It was true. Honestly, she could barely contain herself. If she didn't tell them soon, she felt like she'd burst. "His name is Michael."

"Michael what?"

"Craig. I met him that first night. He recognized me from my picture in the *Chronicle*. We had dinner together."

"That was quick," Margaret said.

"I know. Then he took me to see the floats from the Mardi Gras parade. In a carriage. And we kissed."

"Holy cow," Christie said. "What's he look like?"

Emma sighed again. "Only the most gorgeous man on three continents. Tall, dark, handsome. And his chest. My God."

"His chest?" All three women said it in unison.

"Yeah. His chest." Emma grinned.

For the first time ever, she'd shocked her team into silence. That tickled her.

"I hope this means you're engaged," Margaret said finally.

Emma laughed. "Nope. I'm never going to see him again."

"What? Where is he from?" Jane asked. "Who is he?"

"He's from right here in Houston. But I don't know that much more about him. He's a businessman. Smart. Stunning. The most elegant man I've ever met. It was just, I don't know, magic. A dream. A fairy tale. A once in a lifetime."

Margaret reached over and took Emma's hand. "I'm happy for you—if you're happy?"

Emma nodded. "I know, it's not like me. Not cautious, shy, workaholic me. But I tell you, Margaret, I felt like an honest-to-goodness princess this weekend, and I wouldn't change that for the world."

"Good." The older woman leaned back. "Maybe this will convince you that there's really no need to live like a nun."

Emma picked up her cup and sipped some coffee. "I don't know about that. But it sure is going to be a nice memory."

"Memory, shmemory," Jane said. "I say we find him."

Christie nodded. "Yeah. Why not? I'd bet he'd love to see you again, Em."

"He knows how to find me if he wants to," she said. "But he won't. It's okay. Honest."

Christie and Jane gave each other a look.

"Uh-uh, you guys," Emma said. "No sneaking into the computers. We've got other things to concentrate on. Like the new owners." With that, she stood. "I'm going to see Phil."

"Okay," Jane said, "but we want details when you get back."

Emma nodded. "Wish me luck."

EMMA STRAIGHTENED her skirt and checked her panty hose before she knocked on Phil Bailey's door. His "Come in," was immediate. Ellen, his secretary, had already buzzed ahead.

Emma walked into his office. The large room was an African museum. Pictures and artifacts lined the walls. Maps, only barely conceding the real business of Transco, got one small corner, and that was out of Phil's line of sight. His massive teak desk was neat, but that was only because it was early in the day. By the time Phil left, papers would be strewn everywhere. It was Ellen's lot in life to trail after her boss and keep him out of trouble. Emma wondered if he'd take Ellen with him when he left the company.

"Welcome home," Phil said.

She smiled. "It was a great trip. Thanks. But I understand you've had an interesting weekend yourself." She went over to the leather wing chair in front of his desk and sat down. It was a comfortable chair, and she was at ease. Phil was more than a boss. He was a friend.

She had to admit, he was the one who looked out of place here. Tall, lean, unkempt blond hair, and crooked wire-rimmed glasses had always made her think of him more as a professor than a CEO. He wore suits only when he was going to meet someone from out of the office. Most times, he was in khakis or jeans. Today, he was in his Brooks Brothers.

"Yep," he said. "But don't you worry. You're taken care of."

She tensed. "Taken care of? Does this mean it's a done deal?"

"As soon as I sign on the dotted line. Which should be in about ten minutes."

"But who is this company? What about my team? Are there going to be layoffs?"

He leaned forward and picked up a pen, not to write anything, just to keep his hands occupied. It was a habit of his, and it always told her when he was nervous.

"Your team is safe. You guys are a big part of this company, and frankly, you increased the value. So don't worry."

"What about..."

"There might be some layoffs. But I don't think so. At least not right away. But MRC does things a little differently than I do. They're a big company, and they're going to want to bring in some of their own people."

Emma sat silently for a moment, trying to digest the finality of the decision. She'd worked at Transco for five years. It seemed impossible that things were going to change so drastically.

"Phil, are you happy with your choice?" she asked him.

He looked her in the eyes. "Yeah. It was long past due. No one had offered the right package before. But this time, boy, they nailed every detail. They really did their homework. The kicker was the environmental impact research. I'd never have let it go if they hadn't agreed to keep that intact. With some minor modifications, they are." He crooked his head to the side and stilled his pen. "And they knew about you, too. Your reputation precedes you."

"My reputation? I don't understand."

"You were part of the package, Emma. Without you, there wouldn't have been a deal."

That puzzled her. There wasn't any reason for that. Researchers weren't that uncommon. She liked to pride herself on her job, but really, there was no cause to even mention her in this kind of deal.

The intercom buzzed and Phil picked up the line. "Have him come in," he said, after a moment. He hung up and turned to Emma. "Want to meet your new boss?"

She nodded, and stood. Her stomach tightened. She couldn't help it. This man would have a big impact on her life from now on. She hoped against hope that she'd like him. Of course, he couldn't be another Phil, but maybe he'd be nice in his own way.

The door opened as she turned. At first, all she saw was Ellen. Then he walked in.

And her heart nearly leapt out of her chest.

6

EMMA GRIPPED the back of the chair. She couldn't believe what her eyes were telling her. He was here! He'd come for her! She hadn't known how badly she'd wanted this until she'd turned to see Michael standing at the door.

She started toward him, her heart fairly bursting with happiness. "How did you...?" Something made her step falter. Her question died on her lips. It was his eyes.

They weren't happy or excited. They were cool, guarded. Embarrassed.

She looked from Michael to Phil. Then she got it. A thick lump cramped her stomach and it was all she could do not to fall.

Michael wasn't here to sweep her off to a magic castle. Michael was here because he was the new owner of Transco Oil.

Everything had been a lie. He'd tricked her, seduced her, made love to her, and it was all a lie.

The reality came crashing in around her like a load of bricks.

She'd betrayed the company, sold out her friends, stabbed everyone she cared for in the back. Her stomach clenched again and for a moment, she felt dizzy.

She'd been wrong about him looking guilty. Not a hair was out of place, not a worry line to be seen on his face. Oh, sure, he looked concerned, but she knew what kind of an actor he was. This role should get him an Academy Award. Of course, having a vulnerable stooge like her must have made his job pretty simple.

She couldn't look at him. Not when everything was so raw and real. Not when she could remember so clearly everything he'd done to her, and she'd done to him. She headed for the door, wishing he'd just move so she didn't even have to brush his shoulder.

Instead, he took hold of her arm, stopping her just before she hit the door.

"Wait, please, Emma."

"You two know each other?"

Emma heard Phil speak, but she didn't look back. Jerking herself out of Michael's grasp, she met his gaze. It was a dreadful mistake. For one second she almost believed he felt badly about what he'd done. But what did she know? She'd believed him when he'd said she was beautiful.

She felt hot tears in her eyes and made a run for it. Thankfully, Michael didn't try to stop her again. As quickly as she could, she headed for the ladies' room. Thank goodness it was empty, and she locked herself into a stall and sat down.

The tears came immediately. They burned her eyes, seared her cheeks. The humiliation filled her chest and her heart and she wondered if she was going to throw up. That passed, but it was no kindness. Now she was free to concentrate on what she'd done.

It was her information, she felt sure, that had enabled Michael to make the kind of offer Phil couldn't turn down. She racked her brains, trying to think what it was that had tipped the scales. Talking about how Phil wanted to go to Africa? The emphasis on global protection the company held? Or perhaps it was something less obvious. Something a woman who didn't have stars in her eyes would have seen immediately.

Why? Why had she listened? Why hadn't she trusted her first instincts and told him she wanted to dine alone? And why, dear God, why had she decided to go to bed with him? Her once-in-a-lifetime adventure had turned into a never-to-be-forgotten nightmare. Other women slept around with lots of men. She'd done it once. And this was her punishment.

"Emma?"

Emma heard the door swing closed as Margaret walked into the rest room. She willed her friend to go away, or for the earth to simply open up and swallow her whole. How could she tell Margaret, or Jane or Christie what she'd done? They'd hate her. She already hated herself, why not make it a quartet?

"Hon? What's going on? Ellen just called me. She

said you knew the man who bought the company. That you ran out of Phil's office like you were on fire."

Emma sniffled. She couldn't speak, not yet.

"Em? Are you crying?"

Emma nodded. "Please, Margaret. I can't talk yet."

There was a long stretch of silence. Then Emma heard the door open again.

"What's going on?" Christie asked.

"Is she okay?"

So Jane was here, too. Great.

"She's crying," Margaret whispered, as if Emma weren't three feet away.

"You're kidding? What happened?" Christie knocked on the stall door. "You okay? Want me to get you some water or something? Call a doctor?"

"No," Emma said. "I just want to sit here and cry for a while, is that okay?"

"No, it most certainly is not," Margaret said, adding her fists to the banging on the door. "You come out here right this second and tell us what in blazes is going on. Who is that man?"

Emma dabbed her eyes with toilet paper, and stood up. It was no use. They wouldn't leave her be. She'd have to tell them sometime, so it might as well be now. She opened the door slowly, and saw the three of them standing, waiting, all of them looking concerned.

Once they heard what she had to say, that concern would turn to disbelief. Then to anger. Then worse.

"Come on, Em. Spill." Christie tried to smile at her, but it was a feeble attempt.

Emma steeled herself. Whatever their reaction, she deserved it. She deserved it all. "The man who bought the company is the man I was with this weekend," she said, amazed that her voice didn't crack, and that she didn't fall into a million pieces on the floor. "I'm responsible for the company being sold. I talked. A lot. About Phil, about Transco. I'm sure something I said made the difference."

Margaret, Jane and Christie exchanged confused looks.

"He's the guy you...?"

Emma nodded at Christie's polite query.

"Holy cow."

Margaret walked over to Emma and put her arm around her shoulder. Emma almost shook her off. She wasn't entitled to the comfort. "Now, listen. No matter what you said, you aren't responsible for the company being sold. Phil is the only one who could do that. He's the guy that owns the place, not you."

"But I gave Michael the ammunition, don't you see? If I hadn't shot my big mouth off, he wouldn't have been able to carry this off."

"How do you know?" Jane asked. "This might all just be some coincidence. Maybe he did just see you there, by accident."

Emma laughed. "If you knew Michael, you'd

know that couldn't be true. He planned it all. He..."
She lost it for a moment, and it was Margaret's firm
hold that kept her upright. "He lied to me. But I believed him. I believed every little word. Oh, God, I
slept with him. Do you understand? I went to bed
with him! Me! The nun of Transco."

"Honey, you quit worrying about that. You followed your heart, just like always. There was no way
you could have known he would end up here."

"Oh, Margaret, that's not it. You can't put the
blame elsewhere. I walked into his arms with my
eyes wide open. I threw myself at him, for heaven's
sake."

"So, was he good?"

Everyone stopped and looked at Jane. Then Christie laughed. Margaret's arm shook Emma until she,
too, couldn't hold back. She laughed, and for that she
was grateful.

"Well?"

"He was unbelievable. And the worst part is that
he made me feel...I don't know. He made me feel
beautiful. I thought...just for a minute there, that
someone like him could really..." She couldn't go on.
Her throat clenched up tight and she blinked furiously, trying to hold back fresh tears. It didn't work.

"Well, I think he's an out-and-out bastard," Christie said. "How dare he take advantage of you?"

"He didn't have to work very hard at it," Emma
said, after she'd wrestled back some control. She
looked at her cohorts, each one such a dear friend it

made her ache all over again. "I'm going to miss you guys."

"Where are you going?" Margaret took her arm away, but only so she could meet Emma's gaze.

"I'm resigning, of course."

"Don't be a jerk."

"Thanks, Margaret. That makes me feel all better."

"I mean it. There's no reason for you to quit. You're the best thing about this company. You can bet the bastard knows it, too. Hell, he probably decided to buy the company because he'd get you in the bargain."

"Yeah, right. And you expect me to just carry on as if none of this happened?"

Margaret shook her head. "Honey, I expect you to get even."

"What do you mean?"

"She means," Christie said, nodding, "that you have to stay here. And you have to pay that SOB back."

"How am I supposed to do that?"

"I know," Jane said.

They all looked at her as she leaned oh so casually against the long sink.

"You're going to bring him to his knees, that's how. Make him fall head over heels in love with you, and then you get to dump him straight on his rosy behind."

"Me and what supermodel? Have you guys seen him? Have you seen me?"

All three women gave her a dirty look.

"He's so out of my league, I can't even sit in the cheap seats. I could never get him to fall in love with me. I couldn't even begin."

"Want to bet?"

It was Christie's turn to look smug.

"I don't like that tone of voice," Emma said. "It always leads to trouble."

"Trouble is just what we're looking for, darlin'. You just put yourself in my hands. And watch out Michael. He won't know what hit him."

"You guys are insane, you know that?"

All three women nodded. Despite her absolute knowledge that whatever they were planning wouldn't work, she felt a little sorry for Michael. When the Three Musketeers wanted revenge, they got revenge.

MICHAEL TRIED to concentrate on what Phil Bailey was saying. It was about important, bottom-line figures. But all he could think of was Emma.

The look on her face when she'd seen him was pure devastation. He'd known it was going to be bad, but he hadn't known how bad. And he certainly hadn't realized he was going to feel so guilty. Guilt was a commodity he didn't trade in. It was for suckers and wimps, and he'd exorcised the emotion long ago. Until Emma. Now it was back in spades, and he didn't like it one bit.

He needed to talk to her. But what was he going to

say? A lie formed, ready and available. He could tell her it was all a coincidence, that he'd already made the offer to Transco before they'd met. No, she'd see through it. She was clever and intuitive, which was a large part of the problem.

Especially since he'd decided that he wanted to see Emma again socially. More than socially. Intimately. Something had happened to him over the weekend that he couldn't explain. All he knew was that Emma hadn't left his thoughts. He kept remembering things about her, like the way her skin felt, how she smelled like flowers, the abandon in her voice when they were in bed.

The odds of a repeat performance didn't look good, though. Not after he'd seen her face. But long odds had never stopped him before. With time and patience, he could have her back. All he had to do was figure out how.

"Michael?"

He looked up at Phil. "Yes?"

"Do you need a pen?"

Michael shook his head. "I've got one," he said, and he took his Mont Blanc pen out of his coat pocket. He always signed his deals with this baby. So what if it was a silly superstition. It hadn't done him wrong yet.

He bent to the paper and did a quick scan for any changes in the letter of intent. There were none, which was as it should be. His attorneys and Phil's attorneys had been working nonstop to put this deal together in record time. He would have known this morning if something had gone awry. He wrote his name—only halfway through his signature, the ink in his pen stopped. He tried pressing it harder, but it was no use. It was dry.

Phil handed him his pen, and Michael finished signing, even though a small voice in the back of his head sent warning signals. It was just a pen, just some ink, but what a time to quit on him. Just when he needed all the luck he could muster.

Phil stood and held out his hand the second Michael looked up. "I meant it about the people, Craig," he said. "I've gathered some of the best in the business. It would be foolish not to take advantage of that."

Michael took the man's hand and shook it. "I'm well aware of the caliber of employees here. That's one of the reasons I came to you."

"Good. Then we understand one another."

Michael nodded. "I'd like to walk around a little, get the lay of the land."

"I'll take you."

"No, that's okay. I'm sure you have plenty to do. I'll find what I'm looking for." He took his copies of the contract and put them in his briefcase. "I'll leave this here for now, if I may?"

Phil nodded. "Be my guest."

Michael turned to the door. Just as he walked out, Phil said, "It's down the hall, to the right, then room 114."

Michael didn't stop, didn't acknowledge the words. But now he knew how to get to Emma's office.

EMMA COULDN'T CONCENTRATE. Not when she kept hearing what her friends were up to. Christie was on the phone with the beauty shop. That makeover they'd tried to talk her into was now being scheduled for tomorrow. For once, Emma was going to miss a day at work. A whole day. Maybe, Jane had threatened, two. Because after she was finished with the beauty salon, she was going to see a personal shopper at Dillard's. Although she couldn't afford a whole new wardrobe, she had set aside some money for clothes. Actually, that money had been sitting there for over a year.

She heard Jane talking to the shopper, and the words *sexy*, *hot* and *tight* kept coming up. It was ridiculous, really. Her—sexy, hot and tight? No way. Not with her slender build, B-cup breasts and aversion to high heels.

But the girls had made her promise. What could she have done? There was no choice. She'd betrayed them badly, and all they were asking in return was this flight of nonsense. So she'd agreed.

Margaret wasn't sitting idly by, either. She was on her computer, doing research. Not oil company research. Michael Craig was her target. She was going to find out everything she could about the man.

Knowing Margaret, she'd know his blood type in a matter of hours.

By the time Emma had finished her transformation, Margaret, Christie and Jane would have his dossier finished. There simply were no better researchers in the business, so Emma knew it would be complete. She'd bet a week's pay that they would know not just about his financial status, his car and his house, but about his love life up to and including this past weekend.

They called it ammunition. She didn't know what to call it, except folly. But once they met him, they'd see that for themselves. Then perhaps they could forget about all this and get back to work.

Suddenly, the room grew quiet. Emma looked back over her shoulder and saw that all three women were staring at the door. She followed their gazes. He was there.

"Good morning," he said, his voice cool and firm. "I'm Michael Craig."

Margaret stood up. "What can we do for you, Mr. Craig?" she said, her tone so brittle Emma could practically see the words crackle.

"I wanted to introduce myself, and if I may, have a word with Emma."

He looked at her then, but she couldn't meet his gaze. Her face flushed, and it was too easy to recall the blushes he'd inspired over the weekend. Why didn't he just leave?

"I'm Margaret Castle. This is Christie Perkins and Jane Folley."

Michael walked into the room, and held out his hand to Margaret. She stared at it as if he would give her cooties. Finally, she took it, but just for a second.

He greeted Jane and Christie, too. When that was done, he said, "First, I want you to know that you'll always have a place here. I have no intention of downsizing this department. My people assure me we couldn't do better than you four."

Margaret humphed. But Emma was looking at Christie. She was giving Michael a thorough once-over. Really thorough. Good. By the time he left, everything would be settled.

"Now, I was wondering if I might have a moment?"

Margaret, Christie and Jane all looked at her. She gave a small nod, and the three of them filed out of the room. The looks they gave Michael should have scorched his coat, but he didn't seem to notice. He was too busy looking at her.

They were alone, and Emma's heart thudded in her chest. She still couldn't look at him.

"Emma?"

"What?"

"I want to explain."

Now she did look up. That practiced look of concern, of guilt, was on his face. She wasn't buying it. "What's to explain? Everything seems awfully clear to me."

He approached her, but she scooted farther back in her chair. Taking the hint, he stopped. "It's not what you think."

"No? You didn't purposely introduce yourself to me the other night? You didn't hide the fact that you were trying to buy Transco? You didn't get me to talk about the company so you could put all your ducks in a row?"

He opened his mouth to say something, then closed it again. She saw his chest expand with a deep breath, then he let the air out slowly. "No, that's all true. But that's not all there is."

"I know. I left out the part where I get screwed."

He winced. "You don't understand."

"Sure I do. I may be naive, but I'm not stupid."

"No. I didn't sleep with you because of the deal, Emma."

"Right. You were overcome with lust. I understand."

"Why is that out of the question?"

Her face was still warm, but now more with anger than embarrassment. "Oh, please." She stood up and grabbed her purse from under her desk. "I can see this isn't going to work. I'll have my resignation on your desk first thing tomorrow morning."

When she turned back, he was right next to her. He grabbed her shoulders firmly, and looked her square in the eyes. "Don't. I don't want you to quit. I came in here to tell you I'm giving you a raise. I need you here."

"Oh, that's lovely. A raise? So what does that make me? A company hooker?"

He clenched his teeth and she had to look away. Standing this close to him, she caught his scent. Despite her rage, it softened her insides. His touch burned her, his gaze taunted. There was no way she could work with him, or ever see him again. Not when she felt like this even after she knew the truth.

"You and I had something special, Emma. It had nothing to do with Transco."

"Let me go, please, Mr. Craig."

"No."

"I'm afraid I insist." For a split second, she thought he was going to kiss her. It was absurd, given the circumstances, but there it was. He leaned forward slightly, his lips parted. But that didn't happen. Instead, he let her go. She still felt the imprints of his hands on her flesh.

"I wish you'd reconsider. I know what an asset you are to this company, and I'd like you to stay. I won't bother you. I give you my word on that."

"Your word? Gee, that's comforting."

She walked past him, and didn't stop even when she heard him whisper, "I'm sorry."

7

IT HAD TAKEN THEM until eleven forty-five last night, but Margaret, Christie and Jane had convinced Emma to go along with their plan. As Jane said, "Don't get mad, get even." Frankly, Emma hadn't given in for any such noble concepts. She just figured that two days of shopping and primping would give her time to calm down and think rationally, which she couldn't do at home with her mother looking grave and concerned.

She also had to consider the money. She made a very handsome salary at Transco, and she was pretty sure that she wouldn't be able to meet it if she found a job elsewhere. If it had only been her, she wouldn't have hesitated, but she kept up the house, helped her mother, and of course there was her sister Karen's college tuition.

Although she didn't tell the girls, Emma wasn't going to stay at Transco. She couldn't. It would kill her. But she also wasn't going to be rash. Once she returned to work, she'd start sending out résumés. No sense putting everyone in jeopardy because of her pride. All she could do was pray that she'd find a new position quickly.

Now, as she hung her towel to dry on the shower rod, she took a moment to study herself in the mirror. After today, she wasn't going to look like herself. At least that was her hope. She wished she had time for plastic surgery. She'd like to look different, feel different, *be* different. Anyone but her. Anyone without her memories.

She thought of Michael, and turned from the mirror. Images and snippets of conversation from the weekend had intruded at regular intervals, disturbing in their clarity. But hadn't she set herself up for that? She'd *wanted* to remember everything, hadn't she?

He'd even come to her in her sleep, and that had been the most disturbing thing of all. Because she'd welcomed him. She'd opened her arms and her legs to him. She'd made love with him, and in her dream she had given him everything once more. What did that say about her? Nothing good, she was certain.

She managed to get through her morning rituals, which went quickly as she wasn't supposed to wear any makeup. It felt odd that it was nearly ten and she wasn't at work. Old habits were hard to break. But, according to Jane, she was about to transform from a rather average, kind of skinny, nothing special girl into Mata Hari and Kim Basinger all wrapped up in one. Ha. Not a chance in hell.

MICHAEL HUNG UP the phone and looked at his new office. It was bare now. Phil had taken his African knickknacks and his photos the day before, leaving only the Transco map and the basic furniture. Michael's interior designer was due in a few hours, and she would have it put together in no time. Thank goodness he didn't have to think much about that. Doris had worked for him for the past four years, and she knew his taste, and more importantly, that he didn't want to be bothered about anything but the art.

He reached for his coffee cup, and wondered if it would be too obvious to walk down the hall to Emma's office to see if she'd come in. Although he hadn't received the threatened resignation letter, she hadn't come to work for two days. The women she worked with had clammed up on him, claiming they didn't know a thing. He knew that was garbage. They knew; they just wanted him to suffer.

Women. Why did they insist on rehashing every personal thing about their lives with everyone they knew? He'd have preferred to keep what happened between him and Emma private, but that ship had certainly sailed. Now the research team hated him, and they undoubtedly would spread the word. It wasn't the best of circumstances, but it wasn't insurmountable, either. He'd been involved in plenty of hostile takeovers before. Besides, he wasn't going to be headquartered here for long. Soon Jim Cowling was going to move in and take care of the day-to-day operations.

In the meantime, he wanted to do as much damage repair with Emma as he possibly could. She'd been on his mind more and more. He hated it, but it was the truth. As hard as he tried, he couldn't put the episode aside. She was in him, whether he wanted her there or not.

The most upsetting thing had been his dreams. He rarely remembered them, but for the past several nights he'd awakened to such vivid images he might as well have been looking at a television screen. All the images were of Emma. In bed. Naked, open, willing. Softly pretty, moaning his name.

He stood up and walked out of his office. Grace, his secretary, looked up briefly, then went back to transferring files. He turned left down the hall and walked toward research.

She wasn't there. Margaret and Christie were, though.

"Good morning," he said, after a polite knock that went unacknowledged.

Margaret nodded curtly and Christie just gave him a blank look.

"I was wondering if you'd heard from Emma."

Margaret shook her head. "Nope. Not a word."

"I see."

She turned to her computer and started typing furiously. Michael wanted to ask more questions, but it didn't seem prudent. Even if they had information, they weren't going to give it to him.

"If she does call or come in, please have her get in touch with me," he said.

"Oh, she'll be in touch," Christie said.

Margaret shot her a scathing look, and Christie flushed.

What did it mean? What was Emma planning? It didn't sound good, whatever it was.

"Thank you," he said, as he made his retreat. He took his time walking back to his office, trying to make some sense of that cryptic remark.

"Mr. Craig," Grace said when he got to the reception area. "Someone's in your office."

"Who?"

"Emma Roberts."

His pulse immediately picked up. He had to control himself to walk normally, and not break into a run. He nodded at Grace, then headed toward his closed door. Absurdly, he almost knocked.

Instead, he opened the door. But he was unprepared for what he saw.

It was Emma all right, but not Emma. The woman before him had her features, but what had been done to them made all the difference.

Her long hair was now shoulder length, auburn, silky. Pulled back from a face that he could only describe as strikingly beautiful. Emma had been pretty, but now... His pulse raced heatedly as his gaze moved down; he could actually hear his heart pounding.

The woman was dressed in a suit, but it was a suit that was meant to wield power. Feminine power.

Red. Tight, short skirt. Tailored jacket that emphasized her small waist and the curve of her breasts.

Her legs looked long, which was some kind of trick because he knew she wasn't tall. But those heels—high, spiked, also red—made her legs go on forever.

He moved his gaze slowly back up, until once again he was looking at her face. Even he could see it was just her makeup that was different. A new hairstyle, some mascara and a tight skirt didn't change the fundamentals about her, but he couldn't deny she *had* changed.

There was something in her posture, in her attitude. Something strong, and good Lord, sexy as hell. It was like being hit by a tidal wave, knocked over by a roundhouse punch. He was immediately erect, which did *not* happen to him in a business situation. Especially not in his own office with a woman he'd already taken to bed!

Emma's eyebrow rose. The right one. It went up, and Michael's gaze became transfixed. He found the move erotic in the extreme. It didn't make sense, but try telling that to his johnson.

"Mr. Craig," she said.

Was it possible that even her voice had changed? No. It was his imagination that gave it that smoke.

"You wanted to see me?"

He realized with a start that he'd been staring at her for an inordinately long time. But he was afraid to move, afraid that if he shifted his position, she'd look down and see what she was doing to him. Not that she probably didn't know already. He had a quick image of his face, like a cartoon wolf with eyes boinging out and jaw on the floor.

"I'm glad to see you're—" His voice cracked. Cracked! Like a fifteen-year-old! He coughed. "I'm glad to see you're back," he said, this time normally. But he could feel tiny beads of sweat forming on his forehead.

Jeez, what the hell was happening to him? She'd cast some ungodly spell on him. He'd been preoccupied with her before this...this magic act. Now, he felt consumed. He wanted her. On the desk. Right now.

"Thank you," she said, her tone all business, which just frustrated him more. "What can I do for you?"

"You can tell me if you're planning to stay on here at Transco for starters."

She nodded. Her hair shimmered and moved against her neck. "I'm not planning on leaving. For now."

"I'm glad. I hope I can convince you to stay permanently."

"Nothing's permanent, Mr. Craig."

"It's Michael."

"No. It was Michael. Now it's Mr. Craig."

He nodded, amazed that he was having this conversation at all. He wondered if he should mention the transformation, but then decided against it. He had to remain professional at all costs, even when his blood was boiling.

"Is that all?" she asked coolly. "I have work to do."

He scrambled for something to say. Anything that would make her stay. Lunch, he could ask her to eat with him. No. That wouldn't work. Work. That's it. "I'd like to hear what you're working on now," he said.

"Margaret is finishing up the status report. It will be on your desk by noon. You'll receive one every week."

Dammit. Okay. So she'd won for now. He couldn't think coherently enough to come up with something legitimate to keep her here. "That's fine then. Thank you."

She locked on to his gaze and held it steady. The first trickle of sweat started down his back as time stretched. Was she going to say something? No. What she did was worse. She parted her lips slightly, then moistened the top right corner with the tip of her tongue. He almost groaned aloud.

Emma could hardly believe what was happening. She had him. Really had him. The magic had worked, and damn if she wasn't someone new altogether. This Emma was strong, strong enough to face Michael Craig in his office, to hold her shoulders back, to stand tall and proud and use her sex to her advantage. And what an advantage. She hadn't really believed it until she'd seen his face. But now—

His reaction to the new Emma was painfully obvious. His expensive suit couldn't hide everything. Frankly, she hadn't expected such physical evidence, but she was delighted. It confirmed that what she was feeling inside was showing on the outside.

She also saw that he was sweating. Tiny little beads danced on the edge of his hairline. This was better than she'd ever hoped for. When she'd done the move with her mouth, his gaze had followed every nuance. Just to see what would happen, she moved a little to her left. His gaze moved with her. This was actually getting to be fun. Who would have thought some makeup, a new hairstyle, some flashy clothes could bring about this dramatic a change?

But it wasn't just those things that had made the difference. It was the way she'd felt, still felt, when she'd stepped in front of the mirror at the department store yesterday.

The woman looking back at her had been a stranger. Which was, of course, what made the whole thing possible. Emma couldn't have pulled any of this off. But that woman in the mirror, she could do it. She could do just about anything.

Never in her wildest dreams had she suspected that she could look so...so...sexy. There was no other word. It was as if all her secret longings, her torrid fantasies and wicked thoughts had gone from inside to outside. She was the personification of sex, pure and simple. Oh, she wouldn't cause any traffic accidents on the street, she wasn't that beautiful or anything. But within a certain distance, with a certain kind of man, she could do plenty of damage.

And Michael was that certain kind of man.

It was time to let him go. For now. Later, when she had more time to think about how to wield this new power, she'd hit him again. With each new change over the last two days, she'd found the idea of revenge more and more appealing. After this first foray, she knew she was going to love each and every moment.

Michael Craig was in for some mighty interesting times. She was, as Christie had promised, going to bring him to his knees.

She walked toward him, purposefully in a straight line, as if she planned to walk into him instead of around him. She had to concentrate on not wobbling. The heels were ridiculously high, and she wasn't used to wearing them. But they also made her hips move in a different way, held her shoulders back and her chest thrust out. My God, she felt like a vamp, a seductress. She wanted to laugh out loud!

At the last second, Michael moved. She passed him closely, brushing her shoulder against his. And, what the hell, at the last minute, she stopped by the door and turned. Remembering Lauren Bacall's invitation to Bogie in that old movie, Emma leaned just so, tilted her chin down and said, "If you need anything else, Mr. Craig, just...call."

Then she turned and slunk out of the office. She felt his gaze on her back, well, a little bit lower than her back. It was incredibly hard not to giggle. Wait until the girls got a load of her.

MARGARET DROPPED her coffee cup. The hot liquid splattered all over the gray carpet. Her mouth hung open in what could only be termed slack-jawed amazement.

Christie squealed. So high, it was almost inaudible. Her hands went to her face and she squealed again.

Jane had to sit down. Her words, well, one word, was succinct and heartfelt. Entirely unlike ladylike Jane.

Emma swung the door closed behind her. She turned a little too fast in her high heels and nearly took a header, but caught herself in time. The shoes had to go, but she didn't want to ruin the total effect yet.

"I don't believe it!" Christie said. "You're gorgeous!"

"I suppose that's a compliment," Emma said.

"Yes! I mean, wow! I can't get over it. Turn around. Let's see you from the back."

Emma obeyed, feeling slightly embarrassed, but still flush with the triumph of her scene with Michael.

"Has he seen you yet?" Jane asked.

Emma nodded. "Boy, did he ever."

"Well? Spill."

At the mention of that word, Margaret collected

herself and went to get some paper towels. "I never would have believed it if I hadn't seen it with my own eyes," she said, bringing the roll back with her. "Emma, honey, you are a vision. You've always been a pretty girl, but this is a whole new you."

"I know," Emma said. "Can you stand it? It's like I'm someone else. I *am* someone else. And you know what? It feels great."

"I want the name of that hairdresser," Jane said.

"So, come on. What happened with the bastard?" Christie took the paper towels from Margaret's hand and bent to clean up the mess. Margaret smiled, and sat down.

Emma seated herself on the couch. Her skirt hiked up to the top of her thighs. As she tugged she made a mental note to watch that. She was used to long flowing skirts, not this little tight mini. "He was stunned. I'm not kidding. His eyes nearly popped out of his head."

"I'll bet," Jane said, scooting her chair closer. "I can just imagine."

Emma shook her head. "I don't know, Jane. It was more than I ever expected. He got a... I mean, he..."

Jane's eyes widened. "Honest?"

Emma nodded.

"Holy smoke. Give me the number of the makeup lady, too."

Emma laughed. "The weird thing is, I was good at it. I actually enjoyed making him squirm. It was like being an actress. I was playing this sexy lady, and it felt, I don't know, exciting. I don't know who she is, but she certainly isn't me."

"Whoever she is, she's a knockout." Christie tossed the dirty towels in the trash and sat down next to Emma. "So, what are we going to do with him next?"

"I don't know. I haven't thought past getting through that first meeting."

"I've got some information," Margaret said, turning to her desk. She picked up a file, a thick one. "This, ladies, is Michael Craig. The bastard's whole history. And if I'm not mistaken, we've got all the ammunition we need to lead him quite neatly down the path. Before the month is through, our new boss is going to be begging for Emma's hand. At which time, she'll crush him like a bug."

Emma smiled. She got up and went to her desk, opened the drawer and took out a package she'd brought back from New Orleans. She opened it slowly, and pulled out the voodoo doll. With a careful hand, she wrote one word on the doll's chest. *Michael.*

"Ladies," she said, holding up the effigy. "Let the games begin."

8

MICHAEL RUBBED the sudden pain in the back of his neck as he turned his chair so he could look out the window. The Houston sky looked bluer than it was through the tint, but even so, it was a beautiful day. Wisps of clouds hung over the tops of high buildings and radio antennas. To the east, a jet left a vapor trail.

The pain eased a bit and he sighed. Something had gone terribly wrong here today, and he didn't know what to do about it.

If it had been business, there wouldn't be a problem. Someone out to take one of his companies? No sweat. A company he wanted, that didn't want to be sold? Piece of cake. But Emma?

What was he going to do about Emma?

He still couldn't believe his reaction to her. Nothing like that had ever happened to him before, and frankly, it ticked him off. He'd never been blinded by a woman's skirt, and he had no intention of being blinded now. Emma Roberts had been a pleasant interlude. She was important to the company, and that's why he wanted her to stay. That's it. So why did thinking of her, even now, make him sweat?

The trouble was, aside from Emma, it had been too

long since he'd been with a woman. Simple. He could take care of that with one phone call. He pulled his briefcase over and got his private phone book out. As he flipped through the pages, he eliminated one prospect after the other. Before he knew it, he was on the Zs. Not one of the women appealed.

Damn.

He threw the book in his briefcase and slammed the top down. This was ridiculous. He wouldn't spend another moment wasting his time over this schoolkid infatuation—which was all it could possibly be. Picking up the phone, he got Jim on the line, and started planning for tomorrow's meetings. Come hell or high water, Emma wasn't going to interfere with his day one more time.

THE PORTFOLIO ON Michael was a work of art. Information about his childhood, his school years, his girlfriends, his early business training, were all detailed and meticulous. They didn't call Margaret the terror of the Internet for nothing. She deserved an award.

Emma closed the file, and sat back. She focused for a moment on the way it felt to swing her leg when it was crossed like this. Of course she realized how foolish the thought was. Crossing one's legs was not an event of any importance. But she never had. Not this way, at least. She didn't know why. It must have been the kind of clothes she wore before that made her sit like some prim virgin, knees tight together, ankles delicately crossed.

This was better. A lot better. It gave her that surge of power again, the one she'd discovered this morning. She could imagine sitting in a meeting across from Michael, and swinging her leg like this. He would look, all right. Look to distraction.

She sighed. It was so much easier thinking about tormenting the man than actually dealing with her real problem. She couldn't forget the facts of what she'd done. It wasn't his fault she'd been such easy pickings. He'd just plucked her out, and she'd fallen into his palm like ripe fruit.

No, it was simpler to focus on the revenge. It might not be her finest hour, but when it was over, the deep, overwhelming sense of shame would be gone. Wouldn't it? She prayed it would. And, just as important, she'd be finished obsessing about Michael. Banish him from her thoughts, her dreams. Especially her dreams.

She got her purse and lifted his folder, intending to go over it tonight in a lot more detail. She'd find his Achilles' heel and she'd use it. No mercy. That was her new motto. She'd plan and plot and then when it was all over, she'd be free. She just had to be free.

THE MEETING STARTED precisely at nine. Everyone was there, from Michael, at the head of the table, of course, to Jim Cowling, who was the acting presi-

How to validate your
Editor's FREE GIFT "Thank You"

1. Peel off gift seal from front cover. Place it in space provided at right. This automatically entitles you to receive two free books and a fabulous mystery gift.

2. Send back this card and you'll get brand-new Harlequin Temptation® novels. These books have a cover price of $3.75 each, but they are yours to keep absolutely free.

3. There's no catch. You're under no obligation to buy anything. We charge nothing—ZERO—for your first shipment. And you don't have to make any minimum number of purchases—not even one!

4. The fact is thousands of readers enjoy receiving books by mail from the Harlequin Reader Service®. They like the convenience of home delivery...they like getting the best new novels BEFORE they're available in stores... and they love our discount prices!

5. We hope that after receiving your free books you'll want to remain a subscriber. But the choice is yours— to continue or cancel, any time at all! So why not take us up on our invitation, with no risk of any kind. You'll be glad you did!

6. Don't forget to detach your FREE BOOKMARK. And remember...just for validating your Editor's Free Gift Offer, we'll send you THREE gifts, *ABSOLUTELY FREE!*

GET A FREE MYSTERY GIFT...

YOURS FREE!

SURPRISE MYSTERY GIFT COULD BE YOURS FREE AS A SPECIAL "THANK YOU" FROM THE EDITORS OF HARLEQUIN

PLACE
FREE GIFT
SEAL
HERE

YES! I have placed my Editor's "Thank You" seal in the space provided above. Please send me 2 free books and an exciting mystery gift. I understand I am under no obligation to purchase any books, as explained on the back and on the opposite page.

142 HDL CF3E (U-H-T-03/98)

Name _____

Address _____ Apt. _____

City _____

State _____ Zip _____

Thank You!

dent, to the department heads and support staff. Emma chose her seat carefully. Directly to the right of Michael, close enough to reach out and touch him.

He'd barely looked at her this morning. She was wearing the blue suit, which if anything was more seductive than the red one from yesterday. It was slim and not too tailored, and if she leaned a certain way, the top of her breasts showed under the silky white blouse. She intended to lean a certain way.

But first, she had to get used to the reactions of her co-workers. Jim was no problem as he hadn't met her before, and had nothing to compare with the new look. But the others, my goodness, she felt as though she hadn't merely changed her appearance but her whole personality. It made her wonder what people had thought of her before. Had she really been that much of a Milquetoast? Evidently.

Bob Jamison was practically drooling in his coffee. Ted Williams stuttered twice as much as usual, and his face had yet to get back to its natural color.

The women reacted too, and that wasn't so flattering. Alicia, who had never been a close friend, but always a good companion, had barely said two words to her. Fran Bingle had made a rather cutting comment about the length of her skirt.

Well, it couldn't be helped. She had a job to do, and she was intent on doing it right.

She listened as Michael laid out the agenda. They wouldn't get to her for quite some time, so she was able to plan her strategy. It actually helped that Michael wouldn't look her way.

She took her time. No need to blow the deal by being impatient. An hour and fifteen minutes went by, and that's when she decided to make her move.

She leaned forward, resting her arms so that Michael would get a nice little peek, but no one else would be the wiser. But that wasn't the important thing. What she did next was. She scooted a little closer to him, slipped off her right high heel, and inched her stocking-clad foot toward his leg.

He froze when she touched him. Just froze. He'd been in the middle of a sentence, something about shipping prices. His face colored, not the way Ted's had, but enough. Just pink around his cheeks and a light flush on his forehead.

He continued manfully, enunciating quite clearly, as she moved her foot up. She felt his leg beneath his pants, and she made sure to rub his calf with the ball of her foot.

Michael coughed. He still didn't look at her, though. She smiled pleasantly, enjoying this maybe a little too much. She couldn't wait to see what he did when she hit pay dirt.

Moving slowly, she found his knee, but didn't linger there long. No, the knee held no interest. The inner thigh did.

She took a quick check around the table. No one seemed particularly aware of what she was doing, although Fran had a rather puzzled expression on her face. But she was looking at Michael, not her.

Jim began to speak, and she held her position. Emma didn't want to waste any moves. It wouldn't be half as much fun if Michael wasn't center stage. So she let herself play along the edge of his thigh. Using her toes, and the ball of her foot to tease and touch.

What she hadn't counted on was the heat that started in the middle of her stomach and continued to climb. Her breathing felt a bit shallow, and she could tell she was blushing a little. It was the feel of him, that's all. Perfectly understandable under the circumstances. She wasn't being turned on. That wasn't it.

But as her foot moved, slowly, inch by slow inch, toward the juncture of his thighs, her heart started pounding in her chest. She stopped, not sure she could do it. But then, Michael started talking again.

She swallowed as she steeled her nerves. Then she zeroed in. It wasn't easy. If she hadn't been as limber as she was from all those years of dance class, she couldn't have pulled it off. Thank you, Madame Kieslev.

After a tiny bit of maneuvering, she touched him *there* with her big toe. Immediately, he clamped his legs together, although she doubted he achieved the effect he was after. Her foot was now trapped, right where it was most uncomfortable—for him at least.

His face reddened, and she turned her head to the side so the others couldn't see hers do the same. She couldn't quit now. Especially after discovering just what an impact her little dance was having on him.

He cleared his throat. Ted coughed. Someone got up for more coffee.

Finally, he opened his legs, but instead of letting him off the hook, she moved her foot another inch. Holy cow. He was certainly paying attention. She hoped like hell there wouldn't be a fire in the building, because she doubted very much that Michael Craig could have gotten up right then, even to save his own life.

She had him. Just where she wanted him. And it felt *good*. This seductress business had its moments. This was certainly one of them.

"I think that about wraps it up," Michael suddenly said.

Emma almost dropped her foot. The look on Jim Cowling's face was priceless. His eyes looked like saucers and his mouth hung about three degrees open. Everyone else had similar expressions.

Michael pushed his chair back, dislodging her foot. She thought for a moment he was going to stand, but he didn't. He just stared hard at his team, letting them know that despite the fact that only a quarter of the agenda had been covered, that he himself had been in the middle of making an important point, the meeting was, in fact, adjourned.

"Um, when do you want to pick this up again, Mike?" Jim asked.

"I'll let you know."

A long silence stretched while Emma put her shoe back on. She didn't dare look anyone in the face for fear she'd blush. So she busied herself with her notebook as one by one, the management group left.

When she stood, Michael said, "Not you, Ms. Roberts. I'd like you to stay."

Emma swallowed hard and sat back down. She looked at Fran walking out the door, wishing she had the nerve to just get up and bolt. But she couldn't. He was still her boss. In front of his team, he'd asked her to stay. She was stuck.

The sound of the door closing was way too loud, and it made her jump. She had to get it together, and fast. They were going to talk, and she knew what effect his words had on her. She willed herself to become the new Emma. Crossing her leg helped. Letting her shoe dangle from her toe helped a lot.

"Want to tell me what that was all about?"

Taking one last big gulp of air, then letting it out slowly, she raised her head to look at him. The question in his eyes wasn't merely curious, it was burning.

"Well?"

She smiled a little cat smile. "No, I don't think I do want to tell you what it was about. Why don't you guess?"

He stood up then, unabashed about the state of his trousers, which had a sort of tent-thing going. She graciously kept her gaze on the upper quadrant of his body.

"Okay," he said. "I'll bite. I think you're trying to get a rise out of me, Emma."

She looked down, pointedly.

He sighed. "That's not what I meant."

She looked up again, more pleased than she had any right to be. When she was this Emma, she didn't have any compunction about being a smart-ass. Or about playing her cards out to the last ace.

"So why are you going to so much trouble, Emma? If not to rile me?"

"What do you mean?"

"The hair, the makeup. That suit."

"This old thing? It's been in my closet for ages."

"Liar."

"I beg your pardon."

"You've never had an outfit like that in your life. Up until yesterday. And I think I know why you're wearing it now."

"Do tell, Professor."

He moved closer to her, and it took all her courage not to physically back away. She looked down at her shoe again and tried to remember how powerful she'd felt just moments ago. But when he was right next to her, when she could smell his aftershave, and feel the heat from his body, the new Emma took a header, and it was just the old Emma left to fend for herself.

Her cheeks heated, and so did her solar plexus. She got that feeling back, the one from the weekend.

The electrical charge that he sparked in her whenever he was near.

"I think you want me to fall for you, Emma Roberts," he said, his voice a low, exasperating whisper. He leaned down, his mouth just a breath away from her ear. "I think you want me to want you, so you can tell me to go jump in a lake."

She tried to think. It was hard, what with him being so close. Had the air conditioner stopped working? It was stifling, and she could feel tiny beads of sweat on her neck. She opened her mouth, ready to confess all, when a voice in her head—Margaret's voice—shouted, "Stop!"

Remember what he did to you, Emma. He used you to buy the company. He seduced you so you would tell your secrets. He made you think a man like him...

"Don't be ridiculous," she said, the voice of the new Emma strong and proud and putting him in his place. "I was just amusing myself. I'm surprised you didn't recognize that. You're so good at playing games."

"So it *is* revenge."

"Revenge is such an ugly word."

"But an accurate one."

"If that's what you want to call it, fine."

"What would you call it?"

She stood then, and moved so that her chest was touching his. Not her whole chest. Just the parts he would care about. While she was in the area, she moved her knee, too. Not sharply, as she briefly contemplated, but subtly. Just enough to make contact once more with that most independent of his body parts. He was still paying attention.

"I'd say I'm leveling the playing field, Mr. Craig. Remember, I've got the home court advantage here."

He looked down, capturing her gaze. His eyes were still filled with smoky desire, but there was something else there, too. Something that shook her up a bit more than she liked. A connection, based on a memory they both shared. He'd seen her at her most vulnerable. No matter how many times she managed to tweak his interest, he would always have that on her.

Instead of making her weaken, the realization just made her more determined. He was going to be the vulnerable one. No matter what it took. She'd have that from him.

"What happened to the old Emma?" he whispered. "Is she ever coming back?"

"She's in New Orleans," Emma said. "Playing with pirate ships and Cupids."

"I haven't been able to stop thinking about her," he said, as he moved his hand to her cheek.

His gentle caress made her forget herself for a moment. She closed her eyes. The feel of his flesh upon hers conjured memories that swarmed around and inside her. The bed. His arms. Her moans.

When she opened her eyes, he was still staring at her. Unbelievably, she saw her own want echoed in his gaze. But how could that be? He'd gotten what he'd wanted, hadn't he?

Then she remembered that she'd put that new want there on purpose. She'd worn the suit, cut her hair, walked that walk. What had she expected?

Not this.

Not the ache she saw there now. She'd expected lust, and what he was feeling was so much more.

She knew, because she was feeling it too.

She backed away, needing the distance. But he caught her hand, pulling her right back so she was once again pressed against him.

"Feel that, Emma?"

Of course she did. There was no distance between them at all, and his need was clearer now than ever. Only now, it wasn't just a novel way of keeping score.

"That's what you do to me, Emma. Like this, or like you were in New Orleans. But if I were you, I'd be careful with what you do to me."

"Or what?"

"Or you just might find out what I can do to you."

9

EMMA LOST IT. All her courage, all her determination. Touching him, she had no defenses against the heat in his eyes or the power behind his words. She felt suddenly foolish and helpless, a child trying to play a very grown-up game.

"Let me go," she said.

He didn't budge. If anything, he squeezed her tighter. His mouth opened slightly, and she knew he was going to kiss her. If he did, she might as well throw in the towel. There was only one chance that she could get out of this with even a smidgen of victory. But she had to act fast. One more second, and it would all be over. She had to go on the offensive.

Before his head dipped even an inch closer, she screwed up her courage and kissed him.

She held nothing back. She kissed him with all the power of the dreams he had shattered. She kissed him with the memory of her night as Cinderella. She kissed him as if her lips could wake him from a long night's sleep and set him free.

He didn't stand a chance.

Michael had to pull back. He stepped away from her so that there was a healthy distance between them, and still her kiss lingered. Damn her to hell, she'd done it to him again. She'd caught him off guard, tackled him at the knees. That kiss had turned his mind to mush and crumbled his resolve.

He wanted her so much, he couldn't speak. With her lips moist and open, her eyes wide and challenging, she exuded sex and need and he was no match for its power. There was no doubt in his mind that she could have him any way she wanted him. He'd do whatever she asked. Anything. Step in front of a train, stop a bullet. Anything as long as he could take her in his arms and in his bed and be inside her.

He'd laughed at other men and their sexual obsessions. Called them weak and spineless. Now he understood. There was no choice involved. His need for Emma was as real as concrete and just as unchangeable. With a start, he realized that it wasn't just sex that had him ensnared. It went much deeper than that.

He was mesmerized by the two sides of this enigmatic woman. Her soft vulnerability, and this newly revealed streak of calculating eroticism. The combination was more than he'd ever expected to find in one living, breathing woman. And here she stood in front of him. The only problem was, he couldn't have her.

At least, if she had her way.

"I have to get back to work," she said, and he heard a little shake in her voice.

He knew at the heart of her she was no femme fatale. The wide-eyed girl from New Orleans was inside that Jessica Rabbit body. What he didn't know was if she realized just how successful this act was. He had his doubts. If she knew what he was thinking, she'd be laughing in triumph instead of struggling to maintain her composure.

"Fine," he said. "But remember what I told you. Be careful."

Her mouth tightened. "Thanks for the tip. But I'm not the one who needs to watch my step."

He smiled then. As long as he wasn't too close to her, he could still manage to think logically and effectively. "No? Why don't we see about that?"

Her head tilted to the side as she waited for him to continue. He let her cool her heels for another moment. "Come to dinner with me tonight," he said finally, letting his smile linger as a challenge.

"Are you kidding?"

"You're so confident and in control, I'd think a little dinner would be a piece of cake for you."

Her eyes shifted to the right, then back to his gaze, but only for a second. The problem with the new Emma was endurance. She couldn't maintain the pose when things got dicey. That was good to know.

"It would be. If I wanted to go. But I don't."

"You don't want to? Or you're afraid to?"

"I know you're just trying to bait me."

"Really?"

"Yes. You can't hide those eyebrows, you know."

"Huh?"

"The right one goes up when you play your little games." She pointed to his face. "See? Like that."

He laughed. "My eyebrows are not the body parts you should be wary of."

That one got her. She crossed her arms over her chest. Which wasn't all that good, because it made him look at her cleavage. She wasn't any Anna Nicole Smith, but jeez, in that white blouse she certainly made it clear she was all female. It would have been much easier if he'd never felt the softness of her skin. Or tasted the sweetness of her breasts.

"I'm not wary of any of your body parts."

"No?"

Her gaze skittered to his crotch, then back up again, all in a heartbeat. But he'd seen it. Her blush confirmed the sighting.

"As charming as this has been, I really need to get back to work." She turned to go then, and if he hadn't stepped in her path she would have darted out the door.

"My driver will pick you up at eight."

"I'm not going."

"Wear something..." He took a long, slow look down her body. "Oh, hell. You know what to wear."

"I'm not going."

"Yes, you are."

"Why should I?"

He took one more step closer, even though he knew it was dangerous. All she'd have to do is touch him and his bravado would crumble. His whole plan would backfire. "You'll come because you won't be able to stand not knowing."

She swallowed. Her eyes were dilated and he felt as if he could see right into her. Into her fear, her excitement. An excitement that matched his own.

"Not knowing what?" she asked finally.

"Who's going to win."

"I'M NOT GOING."

"You most certainly are."

Emma gave Margaret her dirtiest look. "Nowhere in your little plans was there any mention of seeing him off the premises."

"It's only dinner."

"It's only dinner with *him*. That's a whole different thing."

"Nothing you can't handle."

"Ha."

"Emma. You can do this. Look what you've done already."

"Made a damn fool of myself. I can't even imagine what the gossip is about me after this morning."

"I haven't heard a thing."

"No one's going to tell you, silly."

"I have my sources."

Emma sighed. That was the truth. Margaret was the most connected human being on the planet.

"So, what are you going to wear?"

Emma put the remains of her sandwich back in the brown bag. She was decidedly not hungry. Truth be told, she was a little sick to her stomach. Thinking about going out with Michael was enough to send anyone to the infirmary. It wouldn't surprise her if she broke out in hives, or suddenly developed a whopping nervous tick.

"Well? What are you going to wear?"

She looked at Margaret, who was just finishing her cold spaghetti. "A uniform."

"What?"

"There's an opening at the McDonald's on Fourth. I'm going to take it."

"Cut it out, Em. I think you should wear black. Didn't Christie say you bought a little strapless number?"

"Would you like fries with that?" she said, practicing. She thought she sounded quite convincing.

"Yes, the black strapless will drive him nuts. And the four-inch heels."

"Would you like to supersize those fries?"

"Maybe wear your hair up. With just a few tendrils falling loose around your face. And don't skimp on the eye shadow."

"How many Happy Meals did you want today?"

"Will you stop it?"

Emma sat back sharply at Margaret's bark. "I'm just rehearsing. Frankly, I think I'd do a great job."

"You're just practicing avoidance."

"Why shouldn't I? Look what I need to avoid!"

"You don't need to avoid one single thing. You have a job to do, and honey, you do it well. Remember how he reacted yesterday? This morning? You've got the man just where you want him. You can't let go now."

"Please let me let go. I'm begging."

"Nonsense." Margaret looked at her sternly. "I don't want to rub salt in the wound, but Emma, the man deserves everything you can give him. Just think about it."

She did, and her spirits went tumbling. The excitement and fear that came with her new identity were excellent diversions. While she was nervous and trying to be brave and sexy, there wasn't room to dwell on the details of her humiliation. That was probably the best part of the whole plan. Now that she'd been jolted back to reality though, the awful memories swamped her. Instead of spurring her on, now all they did was make her want to go home and crawl into bed.

"It's the only way, honey," Margaret said kindly.

"There are other ways."

Margaret reached over and took her hand. "No. This is the only way for you to come out whole."

Emma raised her gaze and met her friend's squarely. "It's too late. I'll never be whole again."

"I don't believe that. And you can't afford to, either. Now, what are you going to wear?"

Emma closed her eyes tightly. Immediately, Michael came to her mind's eye. He was bare-chested, sexy, wanting her. She opened her eyes. "The black strapless number and the four-inch heels."

"That's my girl."

Emma looked down at her hands. "Your girl is scared to death."

"I know, hon. But you don't need to be. You're doing great."

"I don't think I know what that means."

"It means you're taking a bad situation and turning it on its ear. You're not tucking your tail between your legs and running away."

She nodded, but none of that seemed very important at the moment.

"But you want to hear the real reason you're doing this?"

She looked up then, into Margaret's dark brown eyes. "Why?"

"Because all your life, there's been an incredibly dynamic woman trying very hard to make herself known. She's been patient, maybe a little too patient, but I think she knew that someday she'd get her chance to shine. She let you wear your long skirts and your shapeless blouses. She watched quietly as you hid your fantastic brains behind that little-girl shyness. But now, she's not going to be silent anymore. Emma, she...you need to know that 'the new Emma,' as you call it, is you. It's always been you. We've known it for a long time."

Emma felt hot tears well up. One part of her wanted to bolt out of the room, but the other part— the real her, according to Margaret—knew she was hearing the truth. "It's very confusing," she said, her voice a hoarse whisper.

"It doesn't have to be. It might be scary, but that's nothing you can't conquer. Sweetie, it's time you took a stand. Way past time. Don't let this son of a bitch leave you feeling used and tattered. He's not worth it. No one's worth that."

Emma wiped her cheek with the back of her hand. "But if he's such a son of a bitch, why do I still feel this ache inside?"

Margaret shrugged. "Who can say why our emotions take us where they do? Just remember that feelings are feelings. You don't have to act on them. You need to lead with your head on this one, girl. Not your heart. Your heart hasn't done you a lot of favors lately."

"That's for sure."

"Now don't look so sad. Think about how you feel in those new duds of yours. The strength you've found using your feminine wiles. That should pick you right up."

"It does, but only for a while. Then I remember it's me behind the makeup, and it all falls apart."

"Sweetie, it's you on the inside and the outside. Don't sell yourself short."

"I'll try."

"You won't try. You'll *do*. Now, let's get Michael's portfolio out, shall we? I want to go over some data I got this morning. You're gonna love this stuff, Emma. Trust me."

MICHAEL PACED the distance from his dining room table to the far window and back again. If he'd been smart, he would have put on his tachometer about an hour ago. He figured he must have walked a couple of miles already. But he couldn't sit still.

He could just call Eddie. The phone would ring in the front seat of the limo. Emma probably wouldn't even notice. If she was there, that is. But if she was, and she saw Eddie on the phone, she'd know it was him calling, and that he was checking to make sure she was actually there. That would give her an unnecessary advantage. He couldn't do that. Tonight, he needed every ace up his sleeve he could get.

She had it all over him in terms of strategic weapons. Her body alone was the equivalent of a nuclear warhead. That, combined with her anger, made her a worthy foe. Certainly a challenge. But nothing he couldn't take.

And take her is what he intended to do. It was the only thing he could do. Going on like this was completely unacceptable. He wasn't paying attention to business. He had cut an important meeting short. He couldn't eat, he couldn't sleep. It was time to nip this in the bud. Tonight.

He looked at the dinner table, set beautifully by his housekeeper. Candles, bone china, flowers. Perfect. The music he'd selected was slow and sexy. Again, perfect. Champagne chilled in the ice bucket, a dinner courtesy of La Griglia warmed in the oven. The stage was set, ready for the key player to arrive.

His plan was a simple one. He was going to have her in his bed one last time. Finish this game once and for all. Let her know that when she played with Michael Craig, she'd better be playing for keeps.

She'd see that he wasn't a man to be trifled with. He'd get over this ridiculous obsession. He felt sure that once the nonsense ended, the two of them could work together. She'd see that what he'd done in New Orleans hadn't been the crime of the century. Making love to her here in Houston would reaffirm that he hadn't slept with her just to get information. She was a smart woman. She'd understand.

He looked at his watch again. Five minutes had passed since the last time. She should be here by now. Traffic couldn't be that bad. He'd call Eddie. Eddie would be discreet.

Michael went to the phone and lifted the receiver. After he'd dialed the first two numbers, the front door opened. Emma walked in.

All his plans and strategies flew out the window. She'd won, and she hadn't even said hello.

10

IT WAS A MISTAKE. Emma knew it the moment she walked into his apartment. She should never have come. A strapless dress was no match for the man in front of her. Not when he was wearing that tuxedo. If she was smart, she'd just throw her hands in the air right now and cry uncle. She was only human, after all.

She stood by the door and took in the scene as well as she could. Her gaze kept slipping back to Michael, even though Christie had repeatedly told her to get the lay of the land first. She was looking for signs of seduction, and boy did she find them. Champagne, candles, dinner for two.

She hadn't even realized she was going to his apartment until they'd arrived at the building. By then, it was too late to tell Eddie to take her home. Well, okay, it wasn't too late. She could have insisted. But Michael was so close, and she was wearing this dress.

Now she realized she should have left, even if she'd had to walk home. The music alone was enough to suck the bravado right out of her. Gato

Barbieri. The music from *Last Tango in Paris*. Jazz, just as Margaret predicted.

"Come in," Michael said.

She jumped a little. His voice had brought her out of her panic-induced haze. Jane's words came to her, thankfully, so she knew what she had to do. Doing it gracefully was another matter, but since she had no alternate plan, she would give it the old college try.

She smiled, hoping that it came out looking seductive instead of just loony. Then she walked, making sure her chest stuck out and her bottom wiggled. She probably looked like a damn fool, but Jane had insisted. Michael's reaction made her relax a little. Sure enough, his gaze locked on her chest.

If he thought about it even for a minute, he'd realize that her very generous cleavage was courtesy of the WonderBra, and that once that was removed, her boobs would drop like lead weights. She'd pointed that fact out to Jane, who'd simply laughed. She said that men, unless they were under thirteen or senile, didn't care one whit how we went about it, if the end result was big hooters. Jane was a wise woman.

Michael didn't look up until she reached the couch. Then he kind of snapped out of it and blinked several times. His smile faltered, but a second later he got it together. At least as far as she could see. Time would tell.

"Champagne?" he asked.

She nodded. Her instructions were to sip, slowly,

one glass of champagne. No more. No wine. She needed her faculties.

When he turned to open the bottle, she flexed her shoulders. Being a sex kitten was really hard on the back muscles. She also took the time to look around his place.

It was gorgeous. Expensive, she'd expected. That it was this beautiful surprised her. The decor was high art deco, which she'd known from his profile. What she hadn't known was how stunning his taste was, or how very extraordinary his artwork would be. A Tiffany lamp stood on one table, an Erté bronze on another. The paintings on the wall were just a few samples of a much larger collection that he loaned out to various museums. Here he had two Cassandres, both lit exquisitely. She glanced at the table to look at his Lalique crystal. It was far more stunning than she'd imagined.

"You like it?"

He moved next to her soundlessly, the thick carpet muffling his steps. The champagne flute he offered her was also Lalique. She was almost afraid to take it.

"I like it very much," she said. "The whole apartment is wonderful. But I think my favorite is the Frankl." She nodded toward the large set of sky-scraper drawers that was the centerpiece of the north wall.

His brows went up. "You know Frankl?"

She nodded, as if she'd known about the designer since birth. "I'm a fan of deco."

"Really? I wouldn't have guessed."

"Oh? Do I look like I get all my furniture from Kmart or something?"

He laughed. "No. Especially not tonight. You look stunning."

She lowered her lashes, as she'd practiced about five hundred times in the last three hours. "Thank you." While keeping her head down, she raised her gaze. Christie had assured her that the move was seductive without being obvious. All Emma felt was foolish.

Michael raised his glass. "To beautiful things," he said.

She slowly lifted her glass to meet his. The clink seemed very loud to her. She watched as he brought his drink to his lips then drank, his Adam's apple moving up and down in his throat. She shivered, although she wasn't sure why.

"You're not drinking," he said.

She sipped the cold champagne and she suddenly understood all the hoopla about bubbly. It was clear she'd never had good champagne before. This was the nectar of the gods. She sipped again, stopping only when she saw that he was watching her as intently as she'd watched him just a moment ago. Self-conscious, she lowered her glass and walked toward the windows. The whole city was on view from here, and the skyline was breathtaking. At least she assured herself that was what had taken her breath away.

She felt him behind her, and saw his reflection in the glass. The way he looked, handsome as sin and twice as elegant, brought back so many memories from their weekend together that she felt dizzy. Her gaze shifted out of self-defense and she studied herself, a stranger to her own eyes.

Who was she trying to kid? The man had stolen her heart. There, she'd admitted it. It had only been a weekend, but it had been enough. She'd fallen in love with a strange, dark prince, and no matter what she wore or how she did her makeup, she was still just plain Emma in love with a man she couldn't hope to have.

The realization sobered her, but it also made her angry. Why had he done this to her? Made her think, even for a minute, that she could have it all? He had no right to mess up her life like this. She'd been perfectly content until she'd met Michael Craig. Dammit, the man deserved everything she had to give him, and more.

She turned, facing him head-on. "So, you called this meeting. What's on the agenda?"

He looked a little startled. She hoped he was. Keeping him off balance was a primary objective.

"I thought we'd talk."

"I'm listening."

"About that move you made on me this morning."

She laughed. Threw her head back so her hair, which they'd decided two-to-one should be down and flowing, would get all tousled. "That was just to get your attention," she said, still smiling as if feeling him up with her foot was as common as a knock-knock joke.

"It worked."

"And?"

"What do you mean, 'and'? That's what I'm asking you."

She shrugged. "I don't have an and."

"You just wanted to get my attention. In the middle of a meeting. With the whole development team there. Half of whom I'd never met before."

Her grin broadened. "Yep." She sipped her champagne. Twice.

"So, you have it."

"What?"

"My attention. Now, what are you going to do with it?"

She eyed him carefully. "I haven't decided yet."

"Oh?"

She shook her head. "Nope. There are several options. I figure that if nothing else, tonight will show me which one I'm going to take."

"What are these options?"

"Uh-uh-uh. That would be telling."

He opened his mouth, then shut it again. "Have it your own way."

"I intend to."

He reached his hand out and moved a tendril of hair from her cheek. He lingered there, caressing the side of her face. "The games are fine, Emma. For a while. But eventually, you and I need to come to an understanding."

"Really?" She moved her head back, away from the feel of his fingers. She couldn't deal with the distractions. Not now. "And what am I supposed to understand?"

"That when I made love to you, it was personal. Not business."

"Oh, right. I do understand that. Completely."

"I don't think so."

"Why is that?"

"Because you're still angry."

"So if I really understood your motivation, I wouldn't be, is that it?"

He ran a hand through his hair, clearly frustrated. Good. She was doing what she was supposed to.

"No, you'd still have every right. But you wouldn't be angry for the same reasons."

"You amaze me. You honestly think there's any justification for what you did?"

"As I recall, it was totally consensual."

She stiffened. Funny, but it wasn't hard being the new Emma anymore. "It might have been consensual with the man I thought I'd met. But he wasn't going to be my new boss."

"Okay. Fair enough. I was a heel. A louse. I took advantage of the situation. I apologize."

"Oh, honey. If ever a word was too little too late, that has got to be it."

"What do you want, then?"

"Want? I want to go back and live the weekend over. Only this time you'd tell me the truth. This time, I wouldn't be such a trusting fool."

He moved closer to her, so close that she could feel the heat from his body. He touched her face again, but with his palm, cupping her cheek. Before she could stop him, he leaned over and kissed her.

It was a gentle kiss, as sweet and tender as that first night. This was the kiss they'd shared under the pirate ship.

When he pulled back, he held her gaze. "This time, would you come to my bed, Emma? Knowing who I am? What I do? Would you call my name like you did? Would you drive me insane again, Emma?"

No. She wouldn't tell him the truth. She couldn't. If she did, he would know all of this was just an act. A facade to help her stop feeling so ashamed. Because she *would* go to his bed again. She'd go right now if only...

"No," she said. "I wouldn't."

"I don't believe you."

"That's up to you."

"Why won't you admit it?"

"Admit what?"

"That you enjoyed it as much as I did. That we connected."

She sighed and looked at the table, not really seeing, but not looking at him, either. "Fine. I enjoyed it. It was great. An eleven on a scale of ten."

"Come on, Emma. Don't do this."

Her gaze came back to him sharply. "Don't do this? You bastard. You lied to me, you used me to betray my company and my friends, and you tell me not to do this?" She was blowing it, and she knew it. If she didn't stop now, change gears, get her anger under control, everything would be lost.

It took all her resolve, but she did it. She took a deep breath, straightened her back, calmed herself down. The games were just beginning for Mr. Craig. She didn't want her emotions to botch that up. She thought of Margaret's words. Feelings are just feelings.

After one more sip of champagne, she smiled. It felt right. Not forced. "But that's all water under the bridge, isn't it? We have to work together now."

"Right," he said, his eyes narrowed with suspicion. "How come I don't think that's going to be so easy?"

"Maybe because you feel guilty. But don't bother. I've said what I needed to say. As far as I'm concerned, it's over. We don't ever have to bring it up again."

He didn't say anything. He just studied her carefully. The sweet thing was that she wasn't worried about that. He wouldn't see anything to be alarmed about because she felt perfectly calm. More than calm. She was in the zone.

"Now, I thought I was here for dinner," she said.

"Of course," he said, stepping back a little awkwardly. She could tell she'd confused the hell out of him. Good.

"Have a seat," he said, walking over to the table and pulling out a chair for her. "Everything's ready. I just have to get it from the oven."

Her first thought was to offer to help, but she kept her mouth shut. Femme fatales didn't serve dinner. They got served.

She sat down, making sure her skirt rode up her legs just enough to show him that she was wearing thigh-high stockings. That touch was courtesy of Christie, the devil.

When he didn't move for a long moment, she knew he'd seen what she meant for him to see. This was all going according to plan, and unless she blew it again by letting her emotions get the better of her, he would be a puddle of Jell-O by the end of the night.

He coughed softly, then headed quickly to the kitchen. She pulled her chair in, and thought about what she was supposed to do over dinner. First thing was to play with her wineglass.

She took her middle finger and let it glide over the rim. Around and around. Just lightly touching the glass. This was intended to make him aware of her hands. Of her long red nails. According to Jane, this would make him think of other things she could do with her fingers. More personal things.

He came back with two plates, both for her. One a

salad, the other ravioli with a rich cream sauce. It looked and smelled delicious.

She continued doing her thing to the glass. When she looked up, Michael was staring. His eyes had a dreamy look about them, and Emma couldn't help but smile. The girls were too damn good. They ought to write a book.

She stilled her finger and about five seconds later, he blinked. Then he turned and went back to the kitchen, but not before she heard his sigh. She almost felt sorry for him. Almost.

He came back with his salad and pasta. After he put the plates down, he poured them each a glass of deep red wine. Then he looked at her, smiling. "Can I get you anything else?"

She shook her head. "No, this looks wonderful."

"Thanks. I didn't cook it."

"Oh?"

He sat down across from her. "Sorry. Cooking isn't one of my specialties. But I order it well."

"At least you know your shortcomings."

"That I do."

The food portion was next, and Emma tried to remember what it was she had to accomplish. For the life of her, all she could think of was the glass maneuver. She held her left hand down, out of his line of sight, and glanced at it. She'd written a few reminders there, on her palm, just in case. The word *sensual* jarred her memory.

She turned back to Michael. He had his fork in his

hand, but he hadn't started eating yet. He was too busy watching her. He wanted something to look at? She'd be happy to oblige.

Lifting her fork, she brought it to her plate and speared a small piece of pasta. Slowly, very slowly, she lifted it to her mouth as she leaned forward. Michael would have a clear shot of her cleavage, while at the same time he could see her exaggerated movements as she ate the morsel.

It felt awkward as all get-out, but she made sure to pull the ravioli off with her lips, drawing it out as long as possible.

She was able to gauge Michael's reaction immediately. His gaze went from her bust to her mouth and back again. It was almost too easy, really. Like taking candy from a baby. The guy might be a business tycoon and ruthless as hell, but at the core of him he was still a man. God bless testosterone.

She continued eating in just that way, taking her time, occasionally sipping wine or dabbing the corners of her mouth with her napkin. Michael barely touched his food. He didn't speak, and neither did she, but there was so much going on, he didn't seem to notice.

When she was finished, she put her fork down, put both elbows on the table, and leaned even farther down.

Michael put his wineglass down on his spoon and it tipped over. The mess wasn't bad; there had only been a smidgen left, but he jumped up anyway.

To quote Christie, Michael was thoroughly dis-combobulated. On to step two.

"I'll just wipe this up," Michael said, as he headed for the door.

"It was a lovely meal, Michael. Thank you."

"You're welcome. I've got dessert," he called as he disappeared into the kitchen.

"That's okay. I really couldn't eat another thing." She stood up and waited a few seconds, then she bent down and ran her hands up her right leg, pulling her stocking up. She'd timed it perfectly. He came back just as she passed her knee. She didn't look at him. She just concentrated on her position, on giving him the view she wanted him to have. And she didn't stop until she'd pulled the stocking all the way up her thigh, taking the hem of her dress with her.

When she straightened up, she looked surprised, as if she hadn't realized he was there. Damn, but it was fun. His face was pale, his mouth open, the sponge forgotten in his hand.

"I like the music," she said casually, grateful beyond measure she recognized the piece. "I saw Bolling in concert with Rampal."

"You like jazz?" he asked as he started blotting up the wine.

"Of course. Especially the older stuff by Parker and Bessie Smith."

He stopped cleaning for a second to look at her. "They're my favorites."

"Really?"

He shook his head. "How do you like that?" he said, more to himself than her.

"I also like basketball but not baseball. Hockey on occasion." She laughed a little as she walked toward the windows, making sure each step counted. "I hate Hemingway, love Steinbeck and Faulkner. Don't care for chocolate ice cream, but love Hershey Kisses. And I think *The Godfather* was the best film ever made." She turned to him and smiled. "Anything else you'd like to know?"

He tossed the sponge on the table and walked toward her. "It's amazing," he said. "You and I could be twins."

"Not identical."

"No, definitely not." He reached her, moving in past that safe distance that would keep them from touching. Which he did. In one of the slickest moves since Houdini's escape from the straitjacket, he had her in his arms. Pulling her close, he whispered, "I sure do like your taste."

Then he kissed her. And she melted.

11

ROCK HARD AND READY, Michael pressed his body against Emma's, making sure she knew exactly what he had in mind. It wasn't as if he could hide it. The woman had aroused him the moment she'd walked into his apartment. As the evening had worn on, his situation had steadily worsened. It was a peculiar type of torment, one he didn't particularly care for. Not that he didn't like being aroused. He just didn't like being totally unable to control it.

Kissing her wasn't making things better. But he couldn't stop. Not if there'd been a gun pointed to his head. He had to taste her, to touch her. She was a drug and he was completely, irrevocably addicted.

Their tongues danced, their lips meshed, their taste mingled in such a way that it would be forever branded in his mind. Kissing had always been pleasant, but this... This changed kissing forever. It was a new kind of erotic, blending pleasure and pain in a way he'd never felt before. Pleasure from the kiss itself, pain from the reaction it was causing.

He moved his hand to the top of her dress, just to the curve of her pale, silky breast. He moaned as he made contact, teased beyond endurance by the feel of her skin.

She pushed herself slightly forward so his palm cupped her completely. Even though her dress covered most of her, the swell, the curve, the promise of what lay beneath was enough to send him reeling.

Then, oh damn, then she brought her hand to his erection. He struggled not to embarrass himself. He couldn't hold on for long, though. Her fingers played a delicate pattern over the length of him, and even with his clothes lessening the effect, it was just too much. He broke the kiss.

She looked up at him with her smoky eyes, her mouth still moist and swollen from their kiss.

"Come with me now, Emma," he said, barely recognizing his own voice.

She shook her head in slow motion.

"Don't tease me like this. You can see what you do to me."

"I want to," she said breathlessly. "But..."

"But what?" He moved his lower body against her hand. She pressed him firmly, then the hand was gone.

Emma stepped back. She had to. If she touched him once more, she'd give in, and that would spoil everything.

But, holy cow, this was tougher than she'd expected it to be. Tougher than it had any reason to be. Why—if she knew who he was and what he'd done—did she want to make love with him so terribly much? He was a ruthless bastard. He'd hurt her like no one else in her life. And yet she was drawn to him in a way that defied logic, defied reason. He intoxicated her far more than any champagne ever could.

"But what, Emma? Tell me."

"I can't," she said, struggling to remember Margaret's voice. Christie's warnings. Jane's sage counsel.

"I know you want it as much as I do," he said, taking a step toward her.

She backed away. There was a danger zone with Michael. Anything closer than arm's length. Even though the girls had told her to make him suffer, she couldn't. Not any more. Because he wasn't the only one in pain.

She wanted him with her body, but more than that, she wanted him with her heart. This was a job for someone stronger than her. Someone who wasn't a sentimental fool.

"Talk to me, Emma. Don't just leave me like this."

She took a deep breath. She had to carry on. Her pride depended on it. How could she face the team if she caved in now? "I'm sorry, Michael. I'd appreciate it if you called your driver. I want to go home."

The look on his face made her ache. Disappointment, hurt, betrayal and anger were all there, clearly defined in his mouth, and most especially in his eyes. She recognized each emotion. They'd been hers since Monday.

"I thought you said we'd let the past go. That we'd start from scratch."

"I did. I am."

"Then why?"

"I don't think I need to answer that," she said, purposely making her voice stern, even though she felt weak as a baby.

His mouth tightened and she could see his struggle. Absurdly, she wanted to comfort him. Which was decidedly against the rules.

"You want me to court you, is that it? Flowers? Candy? Dinner and a movie?"

She shook her head. "No, that's not it."

"Then what? For God's sake, Emma. Tell me what you want from me. Tell me what I have to do to bring you back."

"I'm not going to sleep with you, Michael."

"Is it because I'm your boss?"

"No," she said, even though that was part of it. It just wasn't the part that mattered.

"It's not because you don't want to. I can see that in your eyes. You can't kiss a man like that and not reveal something."

"Wanting you has nothing to do with it."

He ran a hand roughly over his face. His cool facade, the one she'd been so impressed with when she'd first arrived, was gone now. Left in its place was a man in torment. She'd gotten what she'd come after, so why didn't she feel better? Why was the ache in her chest so heavy?

"What will it take?" he asked, his voice low, desperate.

"I won't make love with you until..."

He moved quickly then, reaching out with both hands to grasp her arms. "Until what?"

She swallowed hard. This was the most difficult moment of all. Not because she was afraid to say the words, but because once she said them, she wouldn't be able to take them back. And once she said them, she'd see just what she meant to him. The real truth this time. She'd know forever that all he'd wanted her for was sex.

Her resolve evaporated, and she knew she couldn't say it. She just couldn't bear to see his reaction. God help her, she still needed the illusion that she could mean something to him.

"Please call Eddie," she whispered.

"You're not going to answer me, are you?"

She shook her head.

He looked as if he wanted to shake her. But he didn't. He just let her go. When his hands left her arms, she wanted them back again. She'd done every single thing according to plan. But she'd lost anyway.

He walked to the phone, lifted the receiver, and then he turned his back on her. The game was over. No hits, no runs, no errors. Just over.

MICHAEL WATCHED the sun rise. A small part of his brain recognized the beauty of the sky, and resented it. He didn't want to see anything beautiful. Not when he felt like this.

Emma had kept him up all night. She'd left shortly after eleven, and he'd opened a bottle of Scotch and planted himself on the couch. His plan to get stinking drunk had never materialized. The booze just wasn't strong enough. He could have polished off the whole bottle, and he wouldn't have felt better.

He kept remembering that one word. *Unless*. Unless what? Unless he apologized? He'd done that already. Unless he sold the company? If that was it, he was in trouble.

He'd made his bed, to coin an unfortunate phrase, and now he was lying in it. Emma could have been his, if he'd played his cards right. If he hadn't used her. The irony was, he could have gotten the company without her information. It would have been a little more expensive, but nothing that would have hurt him in the long run. So it had all been for nothing.

If only he could forget about her, everything would be back to the way it was, and he'd be fine. But forgetting about Emma was like trying to stop breathing. She was just as necessary now. Why? He'd stopped asking that question at three this morning. What difference did it make? The reason wasn't going to get him out of this mess, so there was no profit in dwelling on it. It was enough for him to recognize that he was well and fully hooked. To a woman who would never forgive him.

If she had, if she'd simply brushed aside his behavior, he probably wouldn't be feeling this way right now. Again, ironic. With a little bit of humiliation thrown in for good measure.

He had to shower. Get ready for work. But he didn't want to. That was another problem. If there was one thing he'd been able to count on, it was his honest pleasure in going to work. Emma had taken that, too.

He leaned forward, elbows on his knees, head in his hands. Blaming Emma was only a temporary refuge. She wasn't the villain here. Whatever game she was playing with him, he had no right to complain. But dammit. He'd have to wrap up his work at Transco, and quick, so he could get out of there. Maybe if he didn't see her, or hear her, he'd be able to get her out of his mind. Maybe.

Until he could leave, he'd just have to use some willpower. Stop thinking about her all the time. Get busy, distract himself. There certainly was enough to do at the office. He stood, determined to get through the day without any thoughts of Emma Roberts.

HE BLEW IT the moment he got into the shower. He continued to blow it as he dressed, drank his coffee, drove to work, went over his E-mail, and met with Cowling. She never left him, not even for a short break.

So where did that leave him? Going crazy, that's where. Jim had looked at him as if he was already there. It got so bad, that he'd actually asked Michael if he was feeling okay. The truth was Michael was *not* feeling okay. Michael was feeling like hell. All because of one word.

Unless.

Like a hated song that repeats over and over until you want to scream, the word had invaded his brain, taken over all the higher functions. And still, he couldn't figure out what it meant.

He glanced at his watch. It was nearly three. He hadn't slept in over thirty-two hours. His throat scratched, his muscles ached, and that weird pain he'd been having lately in his neck had bothered him on and off all day. Something had to give. No, someone had to give. And it wasn't going to be him.

He stood, determined to end this garbage here and now. Emma would explain. He'd see to it. He hadn't become one of the wealthiest men in Houston by letting other people call the shots.

He walked quickly out of his office and down the hall, his resolve growing with each step. Emma might have a right to toy with him, but enough was enough. She'd made her point. Now they were either going to get on with it, or let it go. But the games stopped. Period.

Her office door was open. All four researchers were at their desks, working on their computers. Emma looked focused, in control. Well rested. Obviously, she had no trouble keeping thoughts of him at bay.

That hurt. He hadn't known until he'd seen her that he expected her to be feeling as lousy as he did. That turning him down hadn't been an easy choice. Wrong again. Being wrong was becoming a habit with him. At least as far as Emma was concerned.

"Can I help you?"

He turned, jolted out of the mental quicksand by Margaret's curt question.

"No, thanks. I need to speak to Emma."

She didn't look at him. She kept on typing. He waited, none too patiently, until finally she saved her work, then casually turned to face him. Damn her for looking so calm. So beautiful.

"Yes, Mr. Craig?"

"Can I see you for a moment?"

She shrugged. Shrugged! As if it didn't matter one way or the other. Okay, no need to panic. Maybe she was just putting on a good face.

"Margaret, I'll get with you on that Gulf project when I get back."

Margaret looked from Emma to Michael. Her scowl wasn't hard to interpret.

He waited again while Emma took her sweet time getting up. Finally, she was next to him, and then she led him out into the hallway.

He didn't say anything until they'd reached the photocopy room. No need for her cohorts to hear him. He turned to look at her, preparing himself for what he knew was going to be a battle.

"What's on your mind?" she said, as if nothing at all had happened last night.

"I want to talk to you."

"Okay," she said, smiling a little too brightly. "You've got the floor."

He cursed himself for not planning his opening salvo. Knowing how he felt, he should have rehearsed this conversation, made contingency plans for each of her possible responses. "About last night..."

She blushed. Finally, a reaction. He breathed a sigh of relief until he thought about what the blush meant. Was she embarrassed that she'd kissed him? Touched him? Did she regret it? Or was she just pink with the memories of their intimacy?

"I'm sorry," she said, turning her head slightly to the right and looking past him. "I wasn't very fair to you."

That was better. At least she recognized that leaving him with that word dangling like a cartoon bubble over his head was cruel and unusual punishment.

"I left without thanking you for the lovely dinner. I don't know where my manners were."

Michael rocked back on his heels. "What the hell are you talking about?" he said. "I don't give a damn about the dinner."

Her eyes widened and her lips parted in surprise. "My goodness, I was just trying to be polite."

"Screw polite. I want to know what you meant."

"Meant by what?"

"Unless."

"Pardon?"

He felt his anger rise in his stomach like the mercury in a thermometer. "You know what I'm talking about."

"No," she said, far too innocently. "I'm afraid I don't."

"Maybe this will remind you." He stepped up close to her, and took her hand. Making sure she was staring him right in the eyes, he put her hand where it had been last night. Where it was hard, just like it had been last night. Just before she'd said it.

Her blush deepened from pink to crimson. "Michael," she said, only the word came out in a rush of air.

"Yes. Michael. You remember me now, right? You remember what you did. What you said."

She nodded, tugging at her hand. He let her go, shocked himself, now that the flash of madness had passed. "I'm sorry," he said, stepping back from her. "I didn't mean to do that. It was completely inappropriate. I have no business touching you at all." He kept backing away, not sure what he might do next. It was impossible to be near her. He lost his mind around her.

"Wait," she said, reaching out and taking his arm. "Don't go yet."

Now it was his turn to be surprised. He'd have

thought she'd want to be rid of him. As quickly as possible.

"I do know what you mean," she said, looking at him with troubled eyes.

Eyes filled with the kind of pain he recognized all too well. So she had been acting. The realization should have made him feel better, but it didn't. He'd thought he wanted company in his misery. Not so. He wanted to take her pain away, to make her feel better. It wasn't what he expected—a totally new experience. Emma was giving him lots of those. Almost none of them pleasant.

"Michael?"

"Hmm?"

"Why are you looking at me like that?"

"Like what?"

"That. With those eyes?"

He knew what she meant. He just had no explanation. "These are the only eyes I have."

She smiled sardonically. "Touché. I guess I deserved that."

"I didn't say it to be mean."

She looked away. "I know."

"So, will you tell me?"

She didn't turn back for a long time. He breathed deeply, concentrating on the air filling his lungs. It was a relaxation technique he'd learned years ago, but he'd never used it outside of a business context. It helped, but only a little.

When she finally faced him again, the pain and vulnerability were gone. Vanished as if by magic. He

was caught off guard again. Hadn't she just said...
What the hell?

"I'd better get back to work, Mr. Craig. Unless
there's something else?"

He didn't know what to say. His thoughts sput-
tered like a dying engine. Of all the responses in the
world, this was one he would have never guessed.
What had happened in those few moments? What
decision had she made? Clearly it hadn't been in his
favor. He could deal with that. It was this on-off
thing that was driving him batty.

"You're in the wrong line of work," he said, after
he'd regained the power of speech.

"Oh?"

"Yeah. You should work for the FBI. You'd be a
great double agent."

Her shoulders sagged. "Okay. You win. Let's just
stop this now, while we can. I can't do this anymore."

"Stop? Before you've told me?" God, he sounded
so desperate and pathetic.

Emma's struggle was clear on her face. She was
deciding something, again. Something that affected
him deeply, but of course she wasn't going to let him
in on it.

"There's nothing to tell," she said, finally. She
straightened her posture, and he knew that unless he
did something drastic, she was going to keep toying
with him. Well, the hell with that.

"No," Michael said. "I'm not letting you get away
with this."

"I don't think you have a choice."

"I'm not letting you leave until you explain yourself."

She studied him for a moment. "Why is it so important to you?"

"You tell me you won't come to my bed. Unless. And then nothing. You don't think I have a reason to wonder about that?"

Her brows knitted, and she turned her head slightly to the right. The move was familiar now, and that bothered him, too.

"This is more than wondering," she said. "If I didn't know better, I'd think I was more than a means to an end to you."

"You were never that."

"Then what? Why should I go to your bed, Michael?"

He hadn't been prepared for that one, either. He couldn't tell her the truth. That would give her ammunition enough for three world wars. He had to think fast. Use his negotiating skills to put her on the defensive.

He used the only weapon he had. He touched her cheek. Softly. With the back of his hand. "You're so very beautiful," he said.

She closed her eyes and leaned into the caress. Then she stepped back, opening them once more. "No. I won't. I won't let you do that to me. I meant what I said last night. I will not go to your bed. Ever again. Unless..."

And then she turned, and before he could stop her, she ran down the hall and turned the corner.

He ran after her, close on her heels. He almost had her, but she dashed into the ladies' room. He didn't even have to think about it. He just followed her inside.

"This is the ladies' room," Emma said, even though she wasn't surprised that he'd followed her inside. "You can't be in here."

"It's my company. I can do what I want."

"What if someone comes in?"

He went back to the door and turned the metal lock. "Satisfied?"

She shook her head. "I came in here because I wanted to be alone."

"No, you came in here because you wanted to torture me some more."

"Torture you? Don't be absurd."

He walked toward her, and she backed up until her butt hit the long sink counter. The look in his eyes wasn't charitable. In fact, he looked as if he were about to commit murder.

He didn't stop until he'd come so close to her she was forced to lean back a little. He grasped her by the shoulders, and she could feel his anger from his hands through her jacket.

"You," he said, his voice low and dangerous, "are driving me crazy."

She started to say something, but the look he gave her, wild-eyed and warning, made her keep it to herself.

"I can't sleep. I can't work. I can't do anything but think about you and that damn *unless*. I've apologized, every way I know how. I've called myself every kind of fool. I've tried to ignore you, but you won't let me, will you? It's all part of your plot, isn't it? You want me to go insane, right? Well, I won't. Because you're going to tell me. Right now. Aren't you?"

Emma couldn't have been more shocked. The plan had worked! She had him, just as Margaret and Christie and Jane had promised. He couldn't stop thinking about her! It was more than she'd hoped for. Infinitely more. She finally felt ready to tell him. To say the words that would make everything perfect, if he answered correctly. Oh, there was still the fear that he wouldn't. But for the first time she felt as though there was a chance.

Every bit of research they'd gathered on Michael pointed to a negative response. There was nothing on paper to give her any reason to believe she could change that. But then they'd all thought it would take weeks to get him here.

"Well?"

She said one last little prayer. "I won't go to your bed, Michael," she said carefully, aware of the butterflies in her stomach, the constriction in her chest, "unless..."

"Dammit, unless what?"

She'd run out of excuses. She had to say it now, or never. "Unless I'm your wife."

12

EMMA HELD HER BREATH. His face, especially his eyes, would tell her more than his words. In an instant, she had her answer. She let go of her breath...and her dreams.

It had all been about sex. Not love. That was clear from the stark panic she saw written all over his face. Marriage was the last thing on his mind. At least, marriage to her.

When his hands dropped to his sides, she turned, but then she saw his reflection in the mirror. That was worse, somehow. She'd rendered him speechless. Not with her sexy new haircut, or her new clothes, or even her bitch-on-wheels attitude. All it had taken was the hint of a relationship—a real, committed, lifetime love—and he was struck dumb.

"Wife?" he said, his voice so full of confusion she almost laughed.

"That's right, Mr. Craig. I'm sure you've heard the term before."

"But..."

She turned back, forcing herself to concentrate on the anger that still stewed inside. Not anger at him, but at her own stupidity. How could she have ever thought this would turn out happily? Like oil and water, she and Michael didn't mix. He was a Ferrari, and she was a station wagon. Her crush on him was as realistic as having a crush on Tom Cruise. It wouldn't happen. Not in this lifetime.

"Now that that's settled," she said, "I'd better get back to work." She started for the door, but he stopped her, his hand grasping the exact same spot on her arm as before.

"Wait a minute."

"What for?"

"Because we need to talk."

"No, we don't. There's nothing to say."

He pulled her back, forced her to face him. She couldn't look at him, though. She just couldn't.

"You really want me to marry you?" he asked.

If she hadn't been so busy being humiliated, she would have been insulted. "Not anymore."

"Quit it. I'm serious."

"So am I."

"Now come on, Emma. Give me a minute, will you? I mean, that came out of left field."

She nodded, smiling bitterly. "Right. Sex was in the ballpark, but marriage? Completely unrelated. I understand."

"No, that's not what I meant."

"What did you mean?" She studied him now, no longer afraid to see his reactions, or let him see hers. Let him see the fire in her eyes, and let him believe it was there because of him.

"I meant that I just hadn't been thinking along those lines. That's not what our relationship was about."

"Relationship? You call what we had a relationship?"

He sighed and lifted his hands in surrender. "I can't win, can I?"

"Oh, you've won, all right. You have your company. You had me. What's left?"

"Having you again."

"I don't think so. I'm through with being had."

"I didn't mean it that way, and you know it. You're assuming an awful lot. Jumping to some pretty wild conclusions. Why don't you try just being straight with me? Isn't that what you asked me to do?"

"You're right," she said, folding her arms across her chest. "Here's where I stand. I'm leaving Transco as soon as I get any kind of offer I can live with."

"Why?"

Incredulous, she burst out laughing. "Are you really that obtuse?"

"How did this get so complicated, dammit? We had a great weekend together, and don't you deny it. Something clicked between us, and you can't deny that, either. Now we work together, and we have a chance to have a lot more of them. What's so terrible about that? What's the crime?"

"Aside from the fact that you're a lying, conniving

bastard, nothing. It's a great plan. If all I was interested in was sex."

"You were interested last Saturday night."

She winced. "Boy, you sure do hit below the belt."

"I'm prepared to fight as dirty as I have to, Emma." He moved toward her, slowly, as if he were trying to catch a wild creature.

"Why? What's the point?" she asked, stepping back.

"This." He caught her arms and pulled her to him. His kiss was hard and hot and it reminded her of all the things he could do to her. Make her knees weak, her head spin, her heart thud in her chest. And, God help her, make her wet with wanting him.

He didn't let up. His tongue toyed with her lips, then slipped inside her mouth. When he moved his arms around her, pressing her tighter against him, she wondered if he could feel her excitement through her clothes as she could feel his.

It was crazy. Kissing shouldn't do this to a person. It shouldn't do this to her. She had no business running her fingers through his hair, or moving so that she rubbed the hard parts of his body.

He moaned, and she felt the rumble in his chest. His hand found her blouse, and then her buttons. As smoothly as a magician conjuring a silver dollar, he had her jacket open, and then she felt him touch her breast. It was her turn to moan.

His mouth left hers and she gasped. He nibbled on her earlobe, then her neck. "This is why, Emma," he whispered. "Because you make me need you like this."

Her eyes fluttered open. And what she saw made her gasp.

Margaret, Christie and Jane were watching her. Three heads, all in a row, peaked over the bathroom stall doors. Three pairs of eyes wide with shock. Three mouths hanging open.

Michael lowered his mouth to her bra-clad breast. Emma pushed him back, quickly closing her jacket, embarrassment coursing through her just as heat and want had flowed a moment ago.

"What? What's wrong now?"

She saw her three ex-friends duck. "I just..." What was she going to tell him? She couldn't let on about the girls. But she also couldn't pretend that nothing had happened between them. He'd felt her reaction. Lying about it wasn't going to work.

"I can't deal with this now," she said. "When you touch me, I get all confused."

"Welcome to my world."

She had to smile. She really had put him through the spin cycle this morning. "I think we both need time to think," she said. "And to cool down a bit."

"Yeah," he said, scratching his head. "I guess."

"Go on. Get out of here before someone catches you. We'll talk later."

"Promise?"

She nodded. What else could she do?

"And promise me one more thing?"

She glanced at the bathroom stalls. "What?"

"That you won't quit."

"I can't promise you that."

"At least until we have a chance to talk again. Okay? Just till then."

She looked at his face, so earnest, so confused. "All right. At least until then."

He opened his mouth, then shut it.

"What?"

"No, I'm gonna leave while I'm ahead. At least, I think I'm ahead."

She smiled. Then she walked to the door and turned the lock.

True to his word, he didn't say another thing. He just gave her one last puzzled look, then he walked out the door.

Emma waited for a moment, estimating the time it would take him to round the corner and go down the hall, then she turned to face the bathroom stalls. "All right you Peeping Toms. Get out here. He's gone."

Three bathroom doors opened, and Margaret, Christie and Jane walked out. At least Jane had the decency to look sheepish. Margaret and Christie just looked astonished.

"That kiss!" Christie said. "I just about melted, and I was behind a metal door."

"What were you thinking?" Margaret said. "You almost blew it completely. And you had him, right until you let him kiss you."

"I had no idea," Jane said. "Oh, honey, I don't envy you. How are you supposed to fight that?"

"Thanks for the commentary, but why the hell didn't you let me know you were in here?"

"When were we supposed to do that?"

"When I walked in, that's when."

"Michael came in two seconds after you. How were we supposed to know you were going to have sex right there on the sink."

"Margaret, we did not have sex."

"Technically, no. In every other way, you did so."

"Oh, Margaret," Christie said, putting her arm around the older woman. "You've been single too long."

"Oh, hush. You know what I meant. So, what are we going to do now?"

"We?" Emma said. "I think this group experiment is over, don't you?"

"No," Christie said. "It most certainly is not."

"I played my last card. He trumped it. Or weren't you listening to that part?"

Jane shook her head. "Sorry, I have to agree with Christie. This thing isn't over. Not by a long shot."

"It is for me. I resign."

"You can't!" Margaret took her by the arms. "You're inches from winning."

"Winning what? You heard his reaction when I brought up marriage."

Margaret's frown deepened. "Honey, what did you expect? His reaction was just about what we figured it would be. Remember? We planted the seed, that's all. He'll think about it, toy with it. It'll make him look at you with new eyes. That's all."

"Did you want him to say yes?" Christie asked.

Emma heard the incredulity in Christie's voice. Of course they would be shocked. How could they know that her motives had changed? That she no longer wanted Michael's scalp, she wanted his heart. "No, of course not," she said, trying hard to make the words sound like the truth.

"You're in love with him," Jane said, "aren't you?"

Emma tried to deny it. Instead, she had to concentrate on stopping her tears from flowing.

"Even after what he did to you?"

It was no use. She couldn't carry it off. She closed her eyes and nodded.

"Oh, honey," Jane said, her voice filled with sympathy. Or was it pity?

The tears she'd tried to hold back broke free and she turned away from her friends. She didn't want to see the looks on their faces. The contempt. The censure. She already felt enough of those things for herself.

But as she brought the back of her hand to her face to wipe the tears away, she felt hands on her shoulders, and before she knew it she was in the middle of a group hug.

"Stop it, you guys," she said, her voice muffled. "My makeup is getting destroyed."

"The hell with your makeup," Margaret said. "Why didn't you tell us?"

"I had my suspicions," Christie said. "But the clincher was that kiss."

Emma gave them each a tight squeeze and they broke apart. To her surprise, she saw that Jane and Margaret had been crying, too. She smiled weakly. "You don't have to worry. I'll get over it."

"Of course you will," Margaret said. "I'm just sorry you have to go through any of this."

"We just want you to be happy," Jane said.

"It's not like I'm dying or anything," Emma said, her voice finally growing steady. "So don't everybody start wearing black."

Margaret shook her head. "The more I think about it, the more I realize we're on the right track. As long as we can keep the two of you from kissing, this is all going to work out just fine."

"Margaret, what are you talking about?" Emma could hardly believe her ears. Hadn't she understood? The game was over. She was in love with the target. Nothing was going to change that, except time, and perhaps a long stay at a sanitarium.

"I'm talking about taking your life back, Emma. Believing in yourself."

"It's no use. But hey, at least I got a nifty new haircut, right?" She sighed. "To be honest, the game was over before we started. I fell for him the moment he sat down at my table. It was all over but the credits."

"It's not over. Not at all."

"How do you mean?" Christie said. "What's she supposed to do now?"

"Just what she's been doing. Confusing the hell out of him. Making him crazy wanting her."

"To what end?" Jane asked.

Margaret looked at them all as if they were not understanding on purpose. "To walk away with her pride, for heaven's sake."

"Pride?" Emma said. "How am I supposed to get that back? I'm in love with him, and he doesn't love me."

Margaret put her hands on Emma's shoulders and looked her straight in the eyes. "Do you trust me?"

"I'm not sure. Not when you're looking at me like that."

"I'm serious now."

"Okay, I trust you."

"Then will you believe me when I tell you that the worst thing you could do right now is give up?"

Emma sighed. "I'll try. But it's not easy."

"I never said it was going to be easy. Just promise me you won't throw in the towel. That you won't quit. That you'll carry on with the plan, just as if nothing had changed."

"Margaret, you expect too much of me."

"No, I don't. I know you can do this. You're strong, Emma. Stronger than you know."

Emma wanted to say no. To forget the whole thing. But looking into Margaret's confident brown eyes, she couldn't. She'd already disappointed her friend once. She didn't want to do it again. "All right," she said.

Margaret smiled. "Great. Now, go fix your makeup. You have work to do."

Emma looked at the mirror and laughed. "I'll say. I'm a wreck."

"Christie will bring you your purse. Come on girls. Let's go."

Jane gave Margaret a puzzled look. "I don't get it."

Emma heard Margaret's whispered, "I'll explain later." But when she turned to ask what that was about, the girls had gone. She was alone. Alone with the knowledge that she'd agreed to this farce. That Michael didn't love her, and never would. That no matter what happened, the pain in her heart was going to be there for a long, long time.

13

"MIKE, ARE YOU OKAY?"

Michael looked blankly at Jim Cowling. It took him a second to register the question. He nodded, even though he was most decidedly not okay.

He focused on Jim, who was leaning forward in the wing chair across from Michael's desk.

"Let me ask you something. What do you know about Emma Roberts?"

Jim seemed surprised at the question. "Well, she sure as hell wasn't what I expected."

"What did you expect?"

"I don't know. Not her. She's supposed to be the best geographic researcher there is. According to Randy, she's got brains she hasn't even used yet. He also said she was a little on the shy side, but she didn't seem shy to me."

Michael wondered if Jim had seen Emma's footwork the other day. No. He hadn't looked under the table. Maybe he'd guessed, but Michael doubted it. His comments were based on her looks, and that new attitude. There was nothing shy about that.

"Why do you ask? Think she might leave? You

know, I hear Shell wants her. Pretty badly. They've got the money, too."

Michael didn't like that one bit. "Find out what they're going to offer her, will you?"

"Sure thing. Is that it?"

"Hm? Oh, yeah. You have everything you need?"

Jim frowned. "I'm set. But I wonder if maybe you should see a doctor. You look like hell."

"Thanks."

"Hey, I'm just telling you the truth. You haven't looked right since Monday. Is there something you want to tell me?"

"Yeah," Michael said, smiling. "I'm pregnant."

"Very amusing. Really."

"Get the hell out of here, would you, Jim?"

He stood and picked up his briefcase. "We can't afford to have you laid up, buddy. Do yourself and the company a favor. Don't stick your head in the sand. Get a physical. Take a vacation. Do what you need to, okay?"

Michael stood, too. He walked around his desk and put his hand on his friend's shoulder. "Don't worry. I'm not planning to have a heart attack. At least not today."

Jim gave him one last look, then he left, shaking his head the whole way. Michael stared at the door for a long time. His thoughts, of course, were on Emma.

Marriage.

He hadn't anticipated that. He should have—

Emma was a woman, after all. But he hadn't. Maybe because of how they'd met. Or maybe because the "new" Emma didn't look like his, or anyone's, idea of a wife and mother. But now that she'd brought it up, he found himself thinking about the concept. Frankly, it gave him the willies.

He had no intention of getting married. Not now. Not later. Not to anyone. Michael Craig subscribed to the religion of bachelorhood. He'd never confessed this to anyone in his life, but half the reason he was as driven as he was, was because women were attracted to money and power. The combination had been, and always would be, a female magnet. The formula had worked for him for a long time, and he saw no reason to mess with it now. Not even for Emma.

Just for reassurance, he went to his briefcase and pulled out his black book. Filled with numbers of beautiful women, available women, women who could keep a man awake all night. He flipped through the Cs. Toni Chapel. Perfect example. She was twenty-three, six foot two, and she had a thing for the outdoors, and he didn't mean camping. He hadn't seen her in a long time. Maybe she'd like to do a nature hike this weekend.

Picking up the phone, he dialed the first three numbers, then paused.

Toni was a knockout, all right, but he had to face it. She was no Emma.

He hung up, dejected all over again. Not only had

Emma Roberts turned him into a zombie at work, she'd also ruined his sex life. Great. Wonderful. He might as well shoot himself now.

There was only one solution. He had to get Emma out of his thoughts. Out of his brain. Certainly out of his libido. But how? Leave the country? Good idea, except that he'd just bought this company and there was no way he could be away for any length of time for at least six months. Lobotomy? That sounded reasonable. He wondered if his health insurance covered that procedure.

He sat down hard and leaned back in his leather chair. There was a mountain of work on his desk, all things he'd been putting off. He turned his chair so he could look out at the Houston skyline.

Marriage. He'd always seen it as a sucker's deal. Be with one woman for the rest of his life? That would be like eating chicken for every meal forever. Okay, with Emma it would be like eating caviar, but still. Every meal? Every day?

Except…

Emma wasn't like anyone he'd ever met before. It wasn't that she was sexier, although whatever pheromones she produced clearly had his name on them. No, what made Emma so unique was that she was so damned unpredictable. An enigma. He never knew what she was going to do next. He had the feeling that wouldn't change, even if he knew her a hundred years.

She new Frankl. How many women had he been

out with? He wouldn't hazard an estimate. How many had recognized the Frankl design? One. Guess who?

She liked jazz. Okay, so several other women had liked jazz, but Emma liked Charlie Parker!

She was smart. He'd been out with smart women before. As a matter of fact, it was one of his basic requirements. Vacuous females held no interest. But Emma was smart in a way he could relate to. She understood his line of work. She knew enough about business that their conversations were always stimulating. He remembered how they'd talked in New Orleans; Emma had been particularly insightful. He'd thought at the time that she'd be a valuable asset to the company, and his opinion on that hadn't changed. There was no way he was going to let Shell, or any other company, have her. Transco needed her.

He needed her.

He stood up so fast he nearly knocked the chair over. *No.* He was not going to marry her. He didn't give a damn if she was the most exciting woman in the entire world. She was not going to get him to propose. No way. The woman hadn't been born who could make him change his mind about this. He'd never give in. Never.

EMMA SAW Michael's secretary, Grace Porter, sitting alone in the cafeteria. She looked a little lonely, a little bored. Emma lifted her tray—laden with her salad with fat-free dressing, diet cola and slice of cheesecake—and headed toward the woman's table. She wasn't sure why she wanted to talk to Grace. As a matter of fact, she was a little nervous that Grace had heard something too personal for things to be comfortable. On the other hand, Grace had been with Michael for years.

"Mind if I join you?"

Grace looked up, surprised, but smiled easily as she shook her head.

As Emma took the food off her plate, she gave Grace a surreptitious once-over. Quite attractive, Emma guessed she was in her midforties. Neat, precise, but with laugh lines around her eyes and mouth that offset her almost rigid posture. The suit she wore was expensive, a DKNY, if Emma recalled correctly from her recent foray into the world of designer ready-to-wear. Michael had to pay her well.

As she sat, she caught Grace checking her out. Well, tit for tat. It was only fair.

"I'm glad you came over," Grace said, that easy smile once again making Emma feel welcome. "I haven't had time to meet many people here. And if I know the boss, I'll be leaving just after I make some friends."

Emma's chest tightened. Of course she knew Michael wasn't going to stick around, but the words still bothered her. She inhaled, then blew the air out slowly. "How long have you been working with Michael?"

"Close to ten years now," Grace said, shaking her head. "Boy, I can hardly believe it."

"I know what you mean. Time seems to speed up every year."

"Wait till you hit forty. You'll be stunned."

Emma took a bite of salad, barely tasting it. "It must be interesting, though. Working for him."

"It is. My only complaint is that I don't stick around any place long enough for my taste. But moving from company to company has its advantages. I never get bored."

"I'll bet."

"This move, for example." Grace sipped some soda, then ate a bite of fish. "This has been really different."

"How so?"

"Well, there's always a pattern. Mr. Craig is what you'd call a hands-on man. He likes to be on top of things from the start."

"Hasn't he been?"

Grace shook her head. Emma noticed that her short, dark hair was starting to gray, but that it looked rather nice on her.

"No, this one has been different."

Emma wanted to press her, but didn't know how. Was it different because of what had happened in New Orleans? Or different because he'd been as distracted as she'd been?

"For example, last weekend…"

Emma held her breath.

"He was scheduled to come back from his trip on Saturday. Right after he'd made the offer. But he didn't."

"He made the offer on Saturday?"

Grace nodded. "In the morning. He had the plane ready for that afternoon, but he canceled."

Emma's heart beat a mile a minute. She could hardly believe what she was hearing. Michael had made the offer to Phil Saturday morning! Which meant he'd gotten all the information he needed on Friday. Which meant he was with her on Saturday night because...

"I think," Grace said very quietly, "that he stayed because of you."

Emma gasped.

Grace chuckled. "I am his personal secretary," she said, "privy to all sorts of information."

"But how did you...?"

"After ten years, I know the man pretty well, Emma. Something is going on, and all my instincts say that it's because of you."

Emma wanted to ask a million questions, but only one seemed appropriate. "Why are you telling me this?"

"Because I like him. He's a decent man. Oh, he can be ruthless, but he's fair, too. He doesn't take advantage of anyone's misfortune, even though he'd be deeply upset if he thought anyone knew that. When he takes over a company, he tries really hard to make sure no one gets left out in the cold. He doesn't make arbitrary layoffs. He tries to place people in his other companies, if they don't fit where they are."

"But, what he did to me..." Emma stopped, fearing she'd overstepped her bounds.

"I'm not sure what happened between you two, but I will say one last thing. I've never seen him like this before. Never. And, if I were in your shoes, I'd stick around to see what happens. He's worth it."

Emma felt her face heat. She stared at her cheesecake, her thoughts tumbling around in her head so fast she felt dizzy.

Grace checked her watch, then stood up. "I'm sorry I don't have more time to chat, but I've got to get back to work."

Emma managed a smile. "I'm sorry, too."

"I'd like for us to be friends," the older woman said. "I may not be around for long. But then, who knows? Maybe I will."

"I'd like that," Emma said, meaning it. She had a feeling Grace was a good person to know. Not just because of her relationship to Michael, but because she seemed solid and intuitive, two traits Emma respected very much.

Grace put her hand on Emma's shoulder for a second before she left, and the gesture felt very reassuring. But now that she was alone with her thoughts, Emma didn't feel assured at all. Confusion like this made it impossible to think straight. She wanted to leave, to go someplace quiet and peaceful, away from work and Michael and friends, so she could sort things out.

Did her newfound knowledge make any difference at all? It certainly didn't change the fact that Michael had used her to get the company. Okay, so he hadn't slept with her to get that information, but nonetheless, he'd lied to her, and tricked her and no matter how great Saturday night had been, it didn't excuse the rest.

But it also meant that what he'd said about making love had been true. It had been personal, not business. For the first time since Michael had walked through Phil's door, she was able to think about that night without her humiliation completely overshadowing her logic.

She remembered his face as he'd looked at her. The surprise in his eyes, the passion in the set of his mouth, the need so evident she'd been rocked to her toes. What if none of that had been acting? What if it had been real?

Could that possibly mean that Michael had fallen for her, just as she'd fallen for him?

Emma had never believed in love at first sight. Her practical mind could count off a dozen reasons it couldn't be true. Yet it had happened to her. She'd fallen for him the moment he'd sat down at her table, and the rest of the weekend had just cemented her feelings. It was her misfortune to find love for the first time with a man like Michael, but there wasn't anything she could do about it. Except get over him. If that was possible.

Her biggest allies had been the facts. She'd clung to them every time her emotions got the better of her. Hung on to them for dear life. Now those facts were becoming blurred, and she wasn't happy.

If Michael had fallen for her, wouldn't he have answered her differently when she'd brought up the subject of marriage? Would he have dismissed the idea so vehemently?

How could she know? Every bit of research they'd gathered about him pointed to a man who loved his freedom. He had never had a relationship that lasted longer than six months. Mostly, they were brief affairs, and to her surprise, she'd found many of the women he knew continued to date him periodically, even after not seeing him for months at a time.

As soon as she'd heard that, she'd known she wouldn't be capable of doing that. Michael was an all-or-nothing proposition for her. She'd go insane if she had to wait months, heck even days, for him to call.

But why worry about that? Why couldn't she be as cool and casual on the inside as she looked on the outside? She'd hoped that becoming the new Emma would give her the kind of confidence she saw in other women. Take Grace, for example. There's a woman who'd be steady as a rock no matter what.

Or was that a facade, too? Was anyone what they appeared to be? Was Michael? Was he as confused as she was? As uncertain about what to do?

"Grace said I'd find you here."

Emma heard his voice and looked up sharply. Her question of a second ago was answered. Of course he wasn't uncertain. He looked like nothing could shake his firm hold on what he wanted, and how he wanted it.

Just seeing him in his dark tailored suit, his remarkable jaw set in that determined way of his, she got that tightness in her belly that only he could cause. Before this, she'd had to touch him, or at least have been very, very close to him to have this particular reaction. His danger zone was getting bigger. Pretty soon, she imagined she wouldn't be safe in the same state.

"What can I do for you, Mr. Craig?" she asked, sure he knew exactly what he was doing to her.

"Can you spare a moment? I'd like to talk to you in my office."

She shouldn't go. His office wasn't large enough. She'd be in trouble the moment he closed the door. But she stood, anyway.

"Oh, I interrupted your lunch. This can wait."

She looked down at the table. Even the cheesecake had no appeal. "It's all right." They walked together to the door.

They didn't speak as they went down the hall. Her stomach was busy doing flip-flops while she practiced emergency relaxation techniques. He was too close for even one of them to take effect.

At his reception area, she saw Grace, who smiled kindly. Was that a message? Did Grace know why

Michael had come after her? Was there pity in that smile? Oh, God.

Michael stood by the door so she could enter first. She tried to remember to walk the sexy walk, but with her mind such a jumble, she tripped on the carpet. His hand was there to steady her, and that was that. Any illusion of safety evaporated the moment she felt his touch. She was officially a wreck, incapable of coherent thought or speech.

She looked up at Michael, just in time to see a little look of panic in his eyes. He let her go, coughed, walked quickly over to his desk.

"I, uh, wanted to talk to you," Michael said, walking behind his desk, behind his chair. "I have a proposition for you."

For a wild second, Emma thought he meant to propose. It was the word, of course. She realized that in the next second. But still, her heart kept on hammering. Her thoughts kept tumbling. She made her way to the wing chair, and grabbed on to the top of it, fearing she'd do something ridiculous, like swoon. Did people still swoon?

"I've done some thinking about what you said. About...us."

She couldn't say anything. She just nodded.

"I'm not willing to let this go. Frankly, I'm not sure why. But that's not important. The fact is, I want to be with you, Emma. I don't want you leaving the company. I don't want you leaving me."

"I see," she said, but of course, she didn't. What kind of proposition did he have in mind?

"I think I know what you want. I can't give you that, but I can offer something close."

Her grip tightened on the chair. How could he look so calm? So at ease? Then she glanced down, and saw he had the same death grip on his chair that she had on hers. That made her feel a little better, but not much.

"I want you to be my..." He stopped and frowned. "I'd like to set you up in..." Again, he paused, the troubled look on his face deepening. "The arrangement I had in mind was..."

"Are you asking me to be your mistress, Michael?"

At first, he looked relieved. Then when he saw her face, the worry came back. "Yes," he said. "It's not marriage. But it's the best I can do."

In a startling burst of clarity, Emma understood that he was telling her the absolute truth. It was the best he could do. It was more than she had expected, by far. But could she do it? Could she be satisfied being Michael Craig's mistress? The truth was, she didn't know. Even though her instincts said, no, the part of her that ruled her heart told her to wait, to listen. That it was this, or nothing.

"Emma?"

She opened her mouth to say no. But what came out instead was, "All right."

14

MICHAEL WAS STUNNED. He'd never expected her to say yes. He'd wanted her to, but the odds were so great, he'd resigned himself to a bad ending. Emma had agreed to be his mistress!

"Are you sure?" he said, still unable to believe what he'd heard.

She nodded, but the look on her face was as incredulous as his own had to be. He let go of his grip on the chair and walked over to Emma. She looked so very beautiful in her white suit. The long jacket nearly reached the bottom of her short, snug skirt, and below that, those magic legs went all the way down to her white high heels.

He thought of her as his for a moment. Waiting for him eagerly in the new apartment he'd get for her. How he would like to watch her take off that jacket, that skirt. He wondered if her hose were thigh-high stockings. He hoped so.

His gaze traveled back up to her face. The conflict he saw there made him feel ashamed of his erotic thoughts. This was a major deal for Emma. It wasn't minor for him, either. He'd debated the wisdom of asking her to be his mistress for a long while. Back and forth, yes, no. It was a tiny step from mistress to wife, and he wasn't sure he was willing to get that close. But losing Emma—that wasn't to be contemplated.

"Are you sure?" he asked again, this time taking her lovely face in his hands. He caught her gaze, studied her intently. He could see that although she'd said yes, she'd meant maybe.

"Talk to me," he said, letting his hands drop away. Immediately, he wanted the feel of her again, so he took her hands in his.

"I... You just surprised me," she said, her voice a shy whisper.

"You don't have to make up your mind now. Think about it."

"I want..."

"What, Emma? What do you want?"

She withdrew her hands and took a step back. "I want to think about it."

"Remember," he said, smiling a little, "your first instinct was to say yes. That has to count for something."

She smiled back, although it didn't reach her eyes. "I'll remember."

"Okay. We can talk tomorrow, then?"

She nodded. Then she walked toward the door, and he noticed she didn't have that saucy swing to her derriere, even though she was wearing those heels. He liked this walk, too. It didn't seem to matter what she did, how she acted, what she wore. He was entranced with all the Emmas there were. Now, he had to wait, and hope she would once again say, "All right."

"HE ASKED ME to be his mistress."

"He *what?*" Margaret stood up, jostling a stack of papers on her desk and sending them sliding to the floor. She didn't notice.

"He asked me to be his mistress."

"What did he say when you slapped him?"

Emma looked at her toes. "I said yes."

Margaret sat down again. For a very long time, there was nothing but silence in the room. Then the phone rang, making Emma jump. Margaret didn't answer it. Neither did she.

When it stopped, she dared another look at her friend. She sat staring at her with a very worried expression on her face. Somehow, Emma wasn't surprised.

"Now why did you go and do that?" Margaret said, finally. Her voice was soft, almost kindly. Emma would have preferred it if she'd yelled.

"I'm not sure. Maybe because he didn't expect me to. Or maybe because I didn't expect I would."

"Or maybe because you wanted to?"

Emma went to the couch and sat down, slipping off her high heels and tucking one leg beneath her. "I don't know. Honestly, Margaret, I'm so confused my head is spinning. How did I get into this mess?"

"I don't know, honey. All I can think of is that this

guy must be something awfully special if you're willing to go this far."

"He is special. But that's beside the point. What's really got me worried is that I think, for a few minutes there, I was really contemplating being his mistress. Me. Of all people. He doesn't want to marry me. He just wants me around for...well, you know. That's not right. And it's not what I want."

"So, what are you going to do?"

"That's what I'm asking you!"

Margaret shook her head. "I have a feeling I've meddled too much as it is. From this point on, I'm just an interested friend. A neutral friend. Like Switzerland."

"Oh, no you don't. You can't bail on me now. Not after all I've been through."

"But I haven't helped, have I? You're still in a jam."

"If it hadn't been for you and Christie and Jane, I would have quit days ago. I'd be home crying my eyes out, without an income."

"Is that so much worse than what you're doing now?"

Emma sighed. "At least I have an income."

"Can you explain one thing to me?"

Emma looked up. "I'll try."

"What is it about him?"

"About who?"

Emma turned to the door as Christie and Jane walked in from lunch.

"What's going on?" Jane asked. "Anyone want my brownie? If I keep it, I'll just eat it."

Emma shook her head.

"So?" Christie asked, dumping her purse on her desk and flopping into the big chair. "Why do you look like someone's run over your cat?"

"Michael asked her to be his mistress," Margaret said.

"What?" Christie leaned forward and Jane sat down as they both gave the same startled cry at the same time.

"And she said yes."

"What?" Again, the two spoke in a duet.

"Don't get crazy. I'm not going through with it."

"Why not?" Christie said.

"Of course you're not," Jane said, and then looked daggers at Christie.

"Why not?" Christie said again, this time to Jane. "She's crazy about him, and he's nuts about her. So, she won't have a wedding ring. Big hairy deal."

"The big hairy deal is that we're talking about Emma. She isn't mistress material, for heaven's sake. I don't care if she does look like Kathleen Turner in *Body Heat*, she's still our Emma, and she deserves a wedding ring."

Margaret turned to face her young cohorts. "Are you forgetting what the man did? He slept with her so he could buy this company."

"Actually," Emma said, feeling a little left out, "that's not quite accurate."

All three pairs of eyes turned her way.

"I had lunch with Grace today. His secretary."

"We know who she is," Christie said.

"Right. Well, she told me that Michael made the offer to Phil on Saturday morning."

"So?"

"So that means he could have left then. He had what he wanted. But he didn't. He stayed."

"That doesn't make him Saint Peter," Margaret said. "He still used you."

"I know," Emma said, "but it does make a difference. He was with me Saturday night because he wanted to be. Not because he just wanted information."

"What a bewildering decision for a man to make," Margaret said, her voice dripping with sarcasm. "Here's this beautiful woman who's just supplied him with the keys to buying a new company, who's thrown herself at him. Hm. Go back to Houston and work with the attorneys, or stay another night and try and wake Sleeping Beauty with a kiss. Whatever would he do?"

Emma blushed. "It wasn't like that."

"What was it like?"

She closed her eyes and the images from that night came back in a rush. "It was the best thing that's ever happened to me," she said. "It was magic."

"Which brings me back to my question. What is it about him?"

She looked at Margaret. "He listens to me," she said. "Really listens. He respects what I have to say."

"Go on," Margaret whispered, leaning forward so her elbows rested on her knees.

"He makes me feel beautiful. More than these clothes or this haircut. He makes me feel..."

"Sexy?" Christie offered.

Emma nodded. "But there's more to it than that."

"What?" Jane asked.

Emma looked at her hands. "He makes me whole."

Silence. Then Margaret sniffed. "Then that settles it."

Emma risked a peek. Margaret had leaned back in her chair, and had the damn-the-torpedoes look in her eyes.

"That settles what?"

"You're going to have your Michael Craig. And you're going to have him as your husband."

MICHAEL LOOKED at his watch. Three minutes had passed since the last time he'd looked at his watch. It was almost noon and he hadn't heard from Emma.

He'd left word at her office. At her house. At the front desk. But she hadn't called.

So the answer was no. Okay. He'd figured that she was going to change her mind. Why did he need to hear it? Why couldn't he just chalk it up to a damn shame and move on?

At least he'd gotten some work done. Not a great

deal, but some. He knew he was holding everybody up. Jim Cowling was going to call the men in the white jackets soon if he didn't get on the stick. But he couldn't concentrate. Not with this hanging over his head. At the very least, he needed some closure. Real words from Emma's mouth that he could use to silence the hope.

The hell with waiting. He got up and walked out of his office.

"Mr. Craig."

He stopped at Grace's desk. He saw that she'd finished unpacking, and everything in the outer office looked as neat and professional as he could have hoped for. It occurred to him that it had probably been like this for a while, but that he hadn't noticed. "Everything looks great, Grace."

"Thank you. I don't know if I should be telling you this, but I heard something this morning in the ladies' room."

"Yes?"

"Shell has made an offer to Emma Roberts."

Michael's pulse accelerated. He forced himself not to leap over the desk and take Grace by the shoulders. "Oh?"

"It seems she's accepted."

Michael cursed. By the look on Grace's face, he'd cursed aloud.

"I'm sure she'd be amenable to a counteroffer."

"Yes," he said. "Thank you." He walked away before he made a bigger fool of himself. Straight toward Emma's office. By the time he got there, he'd cooled down a little. Not enough. He wondered where the big-time negotiator, the RB of the brief-case, had gone.

He stepped inside, and saw her. Packing. He coughed, just in case the curses running through his head wanted to come out again.

Four heads turned his way. Margaret hung up the phone. Christie and Jane looked from him to Emma, then back again. Emma herself could barely look at him at all.

"So it's true," he said, surprised to see that Emma was wearing a long, flowing dress instead of one of the tight-fitting suits he'd seen her in all week. She looked like the Emma from New Orleans, and that made everything worse.

"I was going to come see you after I finished here," Emma said.

"I thought I had your word."

"Well, sometimes people don't tell the truth. It happens."

He looked pointedly at Margaret. She was quick on the uptake, and herded her two friends out. All three of them gave Emma reassuring pats or glances, which let him know they were all in favor of her leaving.

Once he and Emma were alone, he closed the door. "I thought we were going to talk."

"We can talk now."

"That's a little like closing the barn door, isn't it?"

She put a picture of her mother and sister into the big cardboard box on her desk. "Yes, I suppose so."

"May I ask why?"

She grew still, then she turned to him. "I'm not a mistress kind of gal, Michael. I think we both know that."

"How do you know? You've never tried."

She shook her head. "It's no good, Michael. It wouldn't work. We wouldn't work."

He moved closer to her. "I don't want you to go."

"I can't stay. It wouldn't be fair."

"You think I couldn't handle it? Seeing you every day? I'd never do anything to compromise you, Emma."

"I wasn't talking about you."

That hadn't occurred to him.

She smiled sadly. "We got caught in a little tornado," she said, her voice so gentle and sweet he nearly moaned from the pain of it. "It tossed us all around, making everything crazy. But it's time to settle down now. To get on with it. I can't do that here."

"Don't leave, Emma. The company needs you." He reached out and touched her cheek with the back of his hand, the feel of her a dangerous thing. "I need you."

"No, you don't. You'll see. Once I'm not around, you'll see."

"Here's an idea," he said, knowing he sounded desperate. "Let's start all over. You take some time off, a week, two weeks. Then when you get back, we can take it slow. Get to know each other all over again. See where it leads us.''

''I know where it would lead us. Right here. We want different things from life, Michael. No matter where we start, this is the finish line.''

She was right, of course. That didn't make it any easier.

He looked at her for a long time. Studied her face, her eyes. He'd never forget her, even though he'd need to if he was going to survive.

Then she surprised him. She leaned forward and kissed him gently on the mouth. The softness of her lips did make him moan this time, and his arms went around her of their own volition. He held her tight, never intending to let her go. He kissed her with all his regret, all his need. And she kissed him back.

His hands moved over her body—touching her a needful thing—and he felt her hands do the same frenzied dance.

He pulled back, just for a second, just to look at her, but when he saw the trail of tears on her cheeks, he pulled back for keeps.

''I'm sorry,'' he said.

''Don't be. I'm not going to regret this. I won't. You gave me something magnificent, Michael.''

''What?''

Her gaze met his for what he knew was the last time. ''Me.''

EMMA TRIED very hard to believe. She looked at her friends, Margaret, Christie, Jane and now Grace. Each one of them so hopeful, so certain that everything was going to work out perfectly. She had no such faith.

She remembered how she'd felt in New Orleans, such a short time ago. Like Cinderella. A princess in the making. Sure enough, the prince had come to her door, only the glass slipper hadn't fit. A princess no more, she'd lost her belief in happily every after, despite the best wishes of her fairy godmothers.

"Chin up, Emma. It's going to be fine."

"He's going to find out, Margaret. He's a smart man. He'll check it out."

"No, he won't. Besides, even if he does call Shell, we've got that covered."

"But if he doesn't change his mind, come Monday, I won't have any job."

"Of course you will," Grace said. "Shell really does want you. Although I hope you'll reconsider and stay here."

"If things turn out badly, I won't be able to Grace, but thanks."

Her new cohort smiled. "I know him pretty well, Emma. I don't think you have to worry. The man hasn't done anything but think of you for days. His work is piled sky-high. I tell you, he loves you. It's the only explanation."

"He might love me, but that doesn't mean he wants to marry me."

"You have to remember, he's a guy. Guys are slow on the uptake. He just needs a little push, that's all."

"This is some push."

"Grace is right," Christie said. "Besides, what do you have to lose? You might as well play it out."

"Sure, Em." Jane smiled gamely. "Even I think this is going to turn out right. And you know what a skeptic I am."

"Thank you, guys. Really. I don't know what I would have done without you."

"Go on now, before we all start sniveling," Margaret said, holding out the cardboard box for Emma to take.

She did, grateful for something to do with her arms so she wouldn't be tempted to give them all the big hugs she wanted to. One hug, just one, and she'd fall apart.

Moving quickly, she left the office. The walk to her car was the longest she'd ever taken. She didn't look back. She couldn't. Too much of her heart had been left in that building.

She put the box in the trunk and got behind the wheel. Now what? Home? Her mother would wonder what she was doing there and she'd worry herself sick. She'd want to talk, and Emma wasn't capable of talking right now.

She buckled up, turned the radio on really loud, and headed toward the Cineplex. She was going to lose herself in movies, drown herself in popcorn. Cry herself numb.

MICHAEL GOT THROUGH the entire meeting with Cowling and the department heads. It wasn't easy. Margaret sat on his right, instead of Emma. He kept thinking about the last meeting, when Emma had done that thing with her foot. Despite his best intentions, he found himself growing hard, just remembering.

But he forced his mind—and body—to focus on the meeting, to listen and interact. Margaret kept looking at him strangely, no doubt wondering if he was going to say anything about Emma. He didn't.

When his office was empty once more, he didn't wait, he just dug into his in box, again forcing his concentration to remain steady. Blessedly, three hours passed before Emma came back so strongly he had to put his pen down. At least he wasn't going to lose the company by his inattention. Everything critical had been looked at, if not dealt with.

But now that she was back in his mind, he knew it was useless to go on.

What was he going to do about her? Could he really just let her walk out of his life? Was he prepared to go on as if nothing had happened between them?

The short answer was no. Then what? How could he change the woman's mind? How could he win her back?

He glanced down at his desk, at the prospectus for another company he was in the process of buying.

That's when the idea hit him. Full-blown and tied with a bow.

For the first time in a long while, he smiled. He'd go with his strengths. Use his skills. He'd do what he always did. He'd win.

15

THE LIMO WAS PARKED in front of her house. Of course, she knew it was Michael's. What she didn't know was what she was going to say to him. For a moment, she thought about driving on, finding a motel somewhere and checking in for the night. But that wasn't the plan, was it? Margaret had predicted his arrival, although she'd been wrong on the timeline. He was supposed to show up tomorrow. And she was supposed to have had time to get ready.

It was just after seven, and she'd seen two movies, crying through both of them, even the comedy. She glanced in the rearview mirror, and sighed. She looked as if she'd cried her way through two movies. Puffy, red eyes, blotchy skin, her hair a mess. She'd even managed to spill some soda on her dress. Perfect.

She pressed the button for the automatic garage door and drove in, fervently hoping Michael had waited in the car instead of in the house. Lord knows what her mother and her sister had said to him. Mom had probably dragged out the photo albums. Offered him her terrible coffee. Told him about her arthritis. It was all too dismal to contemplate.

But there was no turning back. She retrieved her purse and stepped out of the car, then went into the house. Her mother was talking in the living room. There was no rest room on her way, so she couldn't stop to repair the damage. Instead, she straightened her back, held her head high, and walked right in.

Only Michael wasn't there. Eddie was.

FOR THE SECOND TIME in a week, she sat in the back seat of Michael's limo, wondering what the night was going to bring. Eddie had opened a bottle of champagne for her, but she didn't pour herself a glass. She wanted to be sober tonight, in control. Not that she wouldn't turn into a quivering wreck the moment she saw Michael, but at least she wouldn't be a drunken wreck.

She looked out the window, not recognizing the street they were on. She supposed Eddie was taking another route to the apartment, but it didn't seem to be a wise choice. They should have arrived about ten minutes ago. Maybe there had been an accident on the freeway, which wasn't at all unusual in Houston.

She shifted on the leather seat, crossing her legs. Once again, she was in the red suit, and she had to pull down the short skirt. There wasn't that same rush of power that she'd gotten when she'd first put on this outfit. If she'd had her druthers, she would have changed into something more comfortable, but she'd decided to stick to the game plan no matter what. That way, when it all fell apart, she wouldn't second-guess herself.

Eddie slowed the limo, and Emma looked outside again. They weren't at Michael's apartment. They'd arrived at a security gate. She tried to find a sign, but Eddie drove on too quickly. Then she got it. It was the planes on the tarmac that gave it away. They were at a small airport.

She leaned forward and tapped on the glass that separated her from Eddie. He pushed the window open. "What can I do for you?"

"Where are we?"

"The Sugar Land Airport."

"Why are we here?"

"So you can have that meeting with Mr. Craig. Like I told you."

"Where is this meeting going to be held?"

"I can't say."

"Can't, or won't?"

"Can't. I just know that I'm supposed to put you on the plane."

"I see. Thank you." She sat back, wondering what she should do. She didn't *have* to get on the plane. She could simply say no. But then what would she have? Unanswered questions, that's what. It didn't matter that she was scared. Hadn't Margaret told her not to let that stop her?

The limo moved up alongside a Learjet, and stopped. A moment later, Eddie opened her door. He held his hand out and she took it, letting him help her. He didn't let go right away, though. "Good luck, Ms. Emma."

"Thank you, Eddie."

He smiled, and walked her to the steps. The closer she got to the door of the jet, the more she felt like Alice about to plunge down the rabbit's hole.

MICHAEL PACED THE FLOOR like a caged tiger. When the hell was she going to get here? It was nearly ten-thirty and if he had to wait much longer, he knew he was going to go crazy.

He'd been calm right up until he'd heard from Eddie that she was on the plane. Since then, he couldn't sit. He couldn't think. All his pep talks about treating this like an unfriendly takeover had flown out the window. Frankly, he was scared to death.

He just knew she wasn't going to change her mind. It didn't matter that they were back in the same suite as the night they'd made love. Or that he'd had the room specially prepared. His speech, which he'd struggled over more than his valedictory address in college, now seemed ludicrous.

Would Emma really care about money? About a fancy apartment? No. She wouldn't. Not Emma. So what was he doing here? It was a mistake. A king-size, gold medal error. She would think he was a fool, or worse.

The thought of losing her all over again chilled him. Dammit, this plan had looked good on paper.

He'd objectively reviewed all the pros and cons, planned for every contingency. Except one. The big one. That Emma wanted it all.

So she was going back to the scene of the crime. New Orleans. She'd finally gotten the information out of the pilot, after she'd reasoned that as soon as she arrived, she'd know where she was. What she hadn't asked was what Michael had been thinking to bring her back there. The pilot wouldn't know. And she wouldn't find out until she was face-to-face with the man in question.

It wasn't fair. But of course, that was the point. Michael knew how she felt about the city. What really bothered her was how those special memories were going to be tarnished. Once tonight had come to its inevitable bad end, she'd have to work hard not to think of New Orleans as the place she'd lost it all.

Didn't he realize she wasn't going to change her mind, no matter the setting? That being his mistress was something she just couldn't live with?

It wasn't as if she hadn't thought it through. My Lord, she'd thought more about this one issue than any other decision she'd ever made. She had pictured herself living in a fabulous apartment, decorated in high deco, of course. She'd seen the gorgeous wardrobe in her closet, imagined her mother and sister taken care of, that burden off her shoulders. Mostly, she imagined Michael coming over. Using his own key. Coming to her bed.

And that's where it got uncomfortable. Where it would always be uncomfortable. She wasn't the kind of woman who could be kept. End of discussion.

"Ms. Roberts, can you please make sure your seat belt is securely fastened? We're starting our descent."

She buckled in tightly. Although the jet was incredibly luxurious, it was small, and that made her nervous. Looking around she realized she hadn't paid enough attention to the jet. She'd been so wrapped up in her own thoughts she hadn't even noticed the outright luxury all around her. The seats alone were noteworthy. Gorgeous tan kid leather, soft and comfortable enough to sleep in, she was forevermore spoiled for coach travel. Everything about the jet was first class. Everything was so very Michael.

Outside, she could see the lights of New Orleans. Her pulse quickened as she tried to spot a landmark. They were still too far away. As they flew lower and lower, she grew more and more certain she wasn't up to this. She would simply tell the pilot to take her back home. That's right. That's exactly what she was going to do.

But she didn't.

When it was time, she got off the plane, just as Michael had known she would.

He surprised her again by not meeting her at the airport. Instead, there was a limousine, navy this time. The driver was a woman. She was young and attractive, and Emma figured she was earning her way through college. Probably doing well, if her service was always this good.

She made sure Emma was comfortable, opened the champagne, poured a glass, turned on the television, adjusted the air-conditioning, then left Emma alone.

It occurred to her that if circumstances were different, she'd have thought of this as a modern-day Cinderella's carriage instead of the car used for funerals.

MICHAEL POURED HIMSELF a glass of champagne, then decided against drinking it. Instead, he called down to room service and ordered up a bottle of Scotch. Why waste time? He'd need to get well and truly drunk tonight, and champagne wouldn't do the trick.

He paced some more, wishing he could take off this damn tuxedo and put on some jeans and a T-shirt. He tugged at the tie, but it didn't loosen. Dammit, he was such a jackass. Maybe he should just get the hell out of here. Leave her a note. Tell her that this was all a gift from him, to say he was sorry. She'd believe that. Why not? He was sorry. Sorry he'd ever dreamed up this wild, stupid scheme.

So what was the alternative? Marry her? Live the rest of his life with Emma by his side? Would that be so terrible?

The short answer was no. It wouldn't be terrible at all. It might even be...

What was he thinking? Hadn't he sworn that he wouldn't give in? That he'd keep his bachelor status no matter what? Even if it meant he'd be miserable without her?

He laughed aloud. For the first time, he got just how ludicrous he sounded. He sat down hard. Damn, but he needed that Scotch.

EMMA STOOD OUTSIDE the hotel, and looked up. He was waiting, in their suite. It wasn't too late to turn back. She could swing by a bank machine and get enough money to buy a plane ticket home. It was the only sure way. If she went up to the room, there was a fifty-fifty chance she'd change her mind. She knew her limitations, even if her friends didn't.

They'd coached her, of course. Told her to make him suffer. Be tough, sexy, seductive. Make him see what he was giving up.

But all she could think about was her own loss. A life without Michael was a high price to pay for her moral convictions. She laughed aloud. Moral convictions, indeed. It was nothing so noble that kept her from agreeing to Michael's proposition. It was her own desire that motivated her, and she knew it. Halfway would never be enough. Where he was concerned, there was no middle ground. Either she would give herself totally, love him completely, no holds barred, or she wouldn't love him at all.

She turned, ready to hail a taxi. But then she remembered her friends. Margaret, Christie and Jane.

The three Musketeers. They'd been so positive. They'd made her promise. How could she let them down now?

THE KNOCK ON THE DOOR startled him. He dug out his wallet, prepared to give the bellman a hefty tip for bringing him the desperately needed Scotch.

He swung the door open, and stopped in his tracks. It wasn't the bellman. It was Emma.

The moment he saw her, all his doubts evaporated like mist in a breeze. She was the most beautiful thing he'd ever seen. This woman, who had captured his heart when he wasn't looking. He wanted to make her happy. To give her the world on a platter. To wake up with her every day, and go to sleep with her every night.

Emma stared at Michael's face, then at the money he was holding out to her. He looked so surprised, she wondered if he was expecting someone else. "What's that for?" she asked.

His eyebrows came down in confusion, then he followed her gaze to his hand. "I thought you were a bottle of Scotch."

"Ah," she said, not knowing what else to say. When he didn't move, she said, "Would you like me to go get you a bottle?"

His brows were still down, but now his right one arched. "A bottle?"

"Of Scotch?"

He gave a little shake of his head, then stuffed the

bill in his pocket. "No, no. Come on in." He stepped back to let her pass.

When she did, it was her time to do eyebrow tricks. Except she wasn't confused. She was stunned! The whole room was filled with flowers. Vases and vases of roses, lilies, mums, daisies, all colors of the rainbow, all breathtaking. The room itself was infused with their soft aroma. Candles flickered on the table, champagne waited in a crystal ice bucket, soft music played over hidden speakers. It was a fairy-tale room, a suite of unexpected beauty and surprises.

She looked at Michael, and his smile told her she'd responded just as he'd wanted her to. It wasn't hard to remember the last time he'd looked at her like that. It was right here, in this city, in another room full of surprises.

"Grace mentioned you liked flowers."

She laughed. "It's gorgeous, Michael, thank you. But..."

"Don't. Wait. I have something to tell you, but first let me get you some champagne."

She nodded. She was in no particular rush to get to the awful part. Even if it was temporary, she wanted to feel good for a little longer.

He poured two glasses of bubbly, and held hers out. She took it, her fingers grazing his lightly. The spark that had always been between them came back in full force. She was tempted to say it was static electricity, but that would be a lie. It was magic, pure and simple.

He knew it, too. She could tell from how he looked at her, how he shook his head, hardly believing what his eyes had seen, what his body had felt. "How do you do that?" he asked.

"It's not me. It's us."

"Us," he repeated thoughtfully, as if the word had a whole new meaning. Then he touched her flute with his own, the clink audible over the gentle music, and brought the glass to his lips.

She joined him, amazed again at how good the sparkling wine tasted. But that was Michael, wasn't it? Sparing no expense. Bringing her the best.

"You look very beautiful, Emma."

She lowered her lashes. Despite the change, the new look, she still found it hard to accept his compliments. "Thank you." She let her gaze travel up his body, remembering with pleasure the tuxedo and how he'd looked the first time she'd seen him. "So do you."

He smiled. "It's hard not to think about that first night, isn't it?"

She nodded, glad he was sharing the memories with her. "I thought you were a paid escort, remember?"

"Right. And I thought you weren't my type."

"Really? You never told me that."

"I figured out my mistake pretty quickly."

He started to move closer to her, but then he

stopped. He stepped back, purposefully, just far enough away so that they wouldn't touch. When he put his glass on the table, Emma's chest tightened, knowing the brief respite was over. It was time for the final goodbye. Just when she was feeling so happy.

"Emma," he said, "I...we..." He shook his head, and took another step back. "I don't know how you do it, but when I get too close to you, I can't think."

"I know what you mean."

He took a deep breath of air.

Emma couldn't stand it. Her heart was about to burst. "Look, it's no good. All the flowers in the world can't make it good. I can't be your mistress, Michael. I won't."

"I know."

She turned from him, unable to look him in the eyes. "Why did you bring me here, then?" His laughter made her turn to stare at him. "I don't see how you can laugh about it."

He sobered, but not all the way. There was still a glint in his eyes, a small upturn at the corner of his mouth. "I'm sorry. It's just that everything has changed."

Now she was really confused. She stepped closer to him, trying to understand what was going on. "Michael, what are you talking about?"

He took in a big breath of air, and let it out all in a whoosh. "Something...happened."

"What? For God's sake, tell me."

"I brought you here to convince you to change your mind. I had it all worked out. Down to the smallest detail. I even had your apartment picked out. In my building, by the way. One floor down."

"But?"

"But now, I don't want it anymore."

Her heart lurched. This was worse than she'd anticipated. At least his words were worse. She couldn't reconcile his expression, though. He looked so darn happy. How could telling her he didn't want her anymore make him that pleased?

"Don't you want to know why?"

She nodded slowly, not really sure she did.

"Because I love you, and I'd like you to be my wife."

She froze. Every cell in her body stilled, not believing what she'd just heard.

"Did you hear me?"

"I don't think so. You want to run that by me again?"

He took a step closer, but still kept an arm's length away. "I said, I love you. I want to marry you."

She tried to speak. But her throat closed up. All she was able to do was make an odd little squeaking noise.

"Emma? Are you all right?"

She nodded.

"Um, would you like to say something?"

She nodded again, but she still couldn't actually

do it. The only thing she did manage to do was cry. Great big tears cascaded down her cheeks.

He took another tiny step closer. "Are those 'Yes, Michael, I'd love to marry you' tears?"

She nodded, willing herself to move, to talk, to rush into his arms. But she didn't take a step.

"Whew. You had me worried there for a minute."

She smiled. Swallowed. "Can I ask you something?" she said, grateful to have her vocal cords back.

"Uh-huh."

"What happened?"

"I woke up. I don't know any other way to explain it. I just knew that letting you go would be the stupidest thing I could ever do. But it was more than that. I don't want you just to stay around. I want you mine. I want to grow old with you. I want us to have kids. Share the bathroom. Go on crummy vacations."

"Are you sure? I don't want you to wake up tomorrow and regret anything."

"Emma, you make me... Damn, it's hard to find the words."

"I make you what, Michael?" she whispered, barely daring to breathe.

He took one more step toward her. "You make me whole."

She closed her eyes, and let the feeling of pure bliss wash over her. He did love her, just as she loved him. When she opened her eyes, she shook her head. "One last question?"

He smiled.

"Why are you all the way over there?"

"I didn't want you to think I was just trying to get you into bed."

She laughed as she swiped the tears from her cheeks. "I believe you."

Then he was there, and she was in his arms. "You've changed everything, you know," he said. "I'm going to have to get a new briefcase."

"What?" She looked up into his beautiful eyes.

"You've turned a perfectly respectable ruthless bastard into a pussycat."

"I wouldn't go that far."

His smile faded, only to be replaced by a look that told her everything. His love for her, his desire, his certainty. "How far would you go?"

"To the ends of the earth," she said.

Then he kissed her.

And she *was* Cinderella.

It's hot...
and it's out of control!

It's a two-alarm Blaze—
from one of Temptation's newest authors!

This spring, Temptation turns up the heat. Look
for these bold, provocative, *ultra*-sexy books!

#679 *PRIVATE PLEASURES*
Janelle Denison
April 1998

Mariah Stevens wanted a husband. Grey Nichols
wanted a lover. But Mariah was determined.
For better or worse, there would be no more private
pleasures for Grey without a public ceremony.

#682 *PRIVATE FANTASIES*
Janelle Denison
May 1998

For Jade Stevens, Kyle was the man of her dreams. He
seemed to know her every desire—in bed and out. Little
did she know that he'd come across her book of private
fantasies—or that he intended to make every one come true!

BLAZE! Red-hot reads from Temptation!

Take 4 bestselling love stories FREE

Plus get a FREE surprise gift!

Special Limited-time Offer

Mail to Harlequin Reader Service®

3010 Walden Avenue
P.O. Box 1867
Buffalo, N.Y. 14240-1867

YES! Please send me 4 free Harlequin Temptation® novels and my free surprise gift. Then send me 4 brand-new novels every month, which I will receive before they appear in bookstores. Bill me at the low price of $3.12 each plus 25¢ delivery and applicable sales tax, if any.* That's the complete price and a savings of over 10% off the cover prices—quite a bargain! I understand that accepting the books and gift places me under no obligation ever to buy any books. I can always return a shipment and cancel at any time. Even if I never buy another book from Harlequin, the 4 free books and the surprise gift are mine to keep forever.

142 HEN CF2M

Name	(PLEASE PRINT)	
Address	Apt. No.	
City	State	Zip

This offer is limited to one order per household and not valid to present Harlequin Temptation® subscribers. *Terms and prices are subject to change without notice. Sales tax applicable in N.Y.

UTEMP-696

©1990 Harlequin Enterprises Limited

THE MEN OF BACHELOR CREEK

Alaska. A place where men could be men—and women were scarce!

To Tanner, Joe and Hawk, Alaska was the final frontier. They'd gone to the ends of the earth to flee the one thing they all feared—MATRIMONY. Little did they know that three intrepid heroines would brave the wilds to "save" them from their lonely bachelor existences.

Enjoy

#662 CAUGHT UNDER THE MISTLETOE!
December 1997

#670 DODGING CUPID'S ARROW!
February 1998

#678 STRUCK BY SPRING FEVER!
April 1998

by Kate Hoffmann

Available wherever Harlequin books are sold.

HARLEQUIN® *Temptation.*

It's a dating wasteland out there! So what's a girl to do when there's not a marriage-minded man in sight? Go hunting, of course.

Manhunting

Enjoy the hilarious antics of five intrepid heroines, determined to lead Mr. Right to the altar— whether he wants to go or not!

#669   *Manhunting in Memphis—* **Heather MacAllister (February 1998)**

#673   *Manhunting in Manhattan—* **Carolyn Andrews (March 1998)**

#677   *Manhunting in Montana—* **Vicki Lewis Thompson (April 1998)**

#681   *Manhunting in Miami—* **Alyssa Dean (May 1998)**

#685   *Manhunting in Mississippi—* **Stephanie Bond (June 1998)**

She's got a plan—to find herself a man!

Available wherever Harlequin books are sold.

Born in the USA

Look for these titles—
available at your favorite retail outlet!

January 1998
Renegade Son by Lisa Jackson

Danielle Summers had problems: a rebellious child and unscrupulous enemies. In addition, her Montana ranch was slowly being sabotaged. And then there was Chase McEnroe—who admired her land and desired her body. But Danielle feared he would invade more than just her property—he'd trespass on her heart.

February 1998
The Heart's Yearning by Ginna Gray

Fourteen years ago Laura gave her baby up for adoption, and not one day had passed that she didn't think about him and agonize over her choice—so she finally followed her heart to Texas to see her child. But the plan to watch her son from afar doesn't quite happen that way, once the boy's sexy—*single*—father takes a decided interest in *her.*

March 1998
First Things Last by Dixie Browning

One look into Chandler Harrington's dark eyes and Belinda Massey could refuse the Virginia millionaire nothing. So how could the no-nonsense nanny believe the rumors that he had kidnapped his nephew—an adorable, healthy little boy who crawled as easily into her heart as he did into her lap?

**BORN IN THE USA: Love, marriage—
and the pursuit of family!**

 HARLEQUIN®   **Silhouette®**

Look us up on-line at: http://www.romance.net

BUSA4

She's a woman without a future
because of her past.

THE DAUGHTER

At fifteen, Maggie is convicted of her mother's
murder. Seven years later she escapes from
prison to prove her innocence.

After many years on the run, Maggie makes a
dangerous decision: to trust Sean McLeod, the cop she
has fallen in love with. She knows he can do one of two
things: he can turn her in or help her find her mother's
real killer. She feels her future is worth the risk....

JASMINE CRESSWELL

Available in April 1998 at your favorite retail outlet.

Available in March 1998
from bestselling author

CATHERINE LANIGAN

Her genius would change the world...

When Karen creates Mastermind, the beautiful computer whiz isn't completely prepared to deal with people's reaction to it. On the one hand, two men have fallen in love with her. On the other, someone wants the program badly enough to threaten her roommate and attack her. Karen doesn't know who to trust—and for all its power, that's the one question her computer isn't programmed to answer....

TENDER MALICE

"Catherine Lanigan is a master storyteller."
—*Rave Reviews*

Coming to your favorite retail outlet.

She's a woman without a future
because of her past.

THE
DAUGHTER

At fifteen, Maggie is convicted of her mother's
murder. Seven years later she escapes from
prison to prove her innocence.

After many years on the run, Maggie makes a
dangerous decision: to trust Sean McLeod, the cop she
has fallen in love with. She knows he can do one of two
things: he can turn her in or help her find her mother's
real killer. She feels her future is worth the risk....

JASMINE
CRESSWELL

MIRA

MJC425

Available in March 1998
from bestselling author

CATHERINE LANIGAN

Her genius would change the world...

When Karen creates Mastermind, the beautiful computer whiz isn't completely prepared to deal with people's reaction to it. On the one hand, two men have fallen in love with her. On the other, someone wants the program badly enough to threaten her roommate and attack her. Karen doesn't know who to trust—and for all its power, that's the one question her computer isn't programmed to answer....

TENDER MALICE

"Catherine Lanigan is a master storyteller."
—Rave Reviews

Coming to your favorite retail outlet.